FOREVER GANGSTA 2

Lock Down Publications and Ca$h
Presents
Forever Gangsta 2
A Novel by *Adrian Dulan*

Forever Gangsta 2

Lock Down Publications
Po Box 944
Stockbridge, Ga 30281

Visit our website @
www.lockdownpublications.com

Lock Down Publications
Like our page on Facebook: Lock Down Publications @
www.facebook.com/lockdownpublications.ldp
Cover design and layout by: **Dynasty Cover Me**
Book interior design by: **Shawn Walker**
Edited by: **Jill Alicea**

Adrian Dulan

Stay Connected with Us!

Text **LOCKDOWN** to 22828 to stay up-to-date with
new releases, sneak peaks, contests and more…
Thank you.

Submission Guideline.

Submit the first three chapters of your completed manuscript to ldpsubmissions@gmail.com, subject line: Your book's title. The manuscript must be in a .doc file and sent as an attachment. Document should be in Times New Roman, double spaced and in size 12 font. Also, provide your synopsis and full contact information. If sending multiple submissions, they must each be in a separate email.

Have a story but no way to send it electronically? You can still submit to LDP/Ca$h Presents. Send in the first three chapters, written or typed, of your completed manuscript to:

LDP: Submissions Dept
Po Box 944
Stockbridge, Ga 30281

DO NOT send original manuscript. Must be a duplicate.

Provide your synopsis and a cover letter containing your full contact information.

Thanks for considering LDP and Ca$h Presents.

PREVIOUSLY...
The Present
KEVIN

I awoke this morning with tears in my eyes. Everything that I dreamt about was the type of things that should keep the average person up at night. Yesterday. a nurse came in to change my bandages and noticed me staring in a daze out my hospital room window. She asked if something was wrong and if I needed any help. I simply played it off like everything was cool and told her that I was just thinking - thinking about the boy; the coyotes; the birds that I'd seen down by the stream. I asked her if I was crazy for thinking that I'd seen that. She laughed and assured me that I wasn't. She told me that when we see things that the mind doesn't understand, our brain goes to work trying to break down the unknown into something that we do understand. When I thought about it, that made sense. What I'd seen down by the stream...didn't.

Several taps at my door drew my attention towards it. "Kevin, how are you feeling this morning?"

I sighed and swiped one hand over my face. Pastor Johnson had returned, except he'd brought someone with him. "I'm still here," I replied. "And the way things are looking, I probably won't be getting outta here anytime soon."

Pastor Johnson nodded in understanding and looked at the man standing next to him. "This is Deacon Jenkins, from the church," Pastor Johnson went on to say. "I told you that I'd be bringing someone with me the next time I stopped by."

Deacon Jenkins walked up and extended his hand for a handshake, but I just looked at it, then looked up at him. Cats like him I don't too much fuck wit'. He reminded me of that snake-ass nigga, Cabbage, except this dude wore dark-tinted glasses, which made it hard for me to see his eyes. He had several gold teeth and wore a suit that was jet black, just like Pastor Johnson's.

We shook hands.

"The pastor has told me a lot about you," Deacon Jenkins began by saying as he pulled up a chair alongside my bed. "I figured it must be God's will that I stop by and have a word with you, especially, being that it was on my heart to do so."

I shot Pastor Johnson a sideways look before returning my gaze back to Deacon Jenkins. "I told the pastor that I wasn't ready to meet with anyone," I replied. "If he told you anything about me, then you should know that now wasn't the time for this."

Deacon Jenkins smiled and sat down, despite what I'd just told him. Pastor Johnson strolled across the room and sat down in a chair by the window. I looked back and forth between they asses like they were crazy.

"Every day is the time for what I came to bear witness of," Deacon Jenkins went on to say.

"Haven't we all heard that one before?" I asked sarcastically. "Don't get me wrong, I ain't knockin' nothing that y'all are trying to do. I get it. I'm going to hell if I don't do what y'all tell me to."

"Who told you that?"

"Deacon, please. I have too much going on to be playing these games with you. I got the Feds snooping around, asking questions. Detectives stop by here every hour on the hour. I have problems sleeping at night, and now this."

"I'm not here to do what those other people have been doing to you, Kevin. I'm here to help you understand why you're here. You're in a dark place; a state of confusion. I want you to see the light. I want you to understand."

I slowly shook my head and replied, "And just how do you think you're going to help me understand? I guess you're going to open your bible and read me some ancient-ass story about some shit that don't have nothing to do with me. Then, I suppose you're going to take that same story, turn it around and make it out to fit the situation that I'm dealing with?"

"No, I'm going to tell you a little about me. I'm going to use my trials and tribulations as a testimony of God's Grace. We have a whole lot more in common than you think we do, Kevin."

"Oh, we do? I don't think you have people chasing you around trying to kill you. And I damn sure don't think you had to stand by and watch someone you love get gunned down."

"I might not have people trying to kill me, now. But that's not to say that I haven't dealt with that problem in the past. Do you think that you're the only person in the world that has had something tragic happen to them because of their dealings with the streets?"

I simply sat there and mugged his ass. I already told them dudes that now wasn't the time. The fuck I look like being nice and entertaining his sarcastic remarks?

Deacon Jenkins chuckled and said, "Sadly, if you think you're the only one that has been victimized because of your dealings in the streets, then you're mistaken. When I told you that we have a lot in common, it's because we do. We both chose to go through this thing called life the hard way. We chose the streets. But what you've failed to understand is, when we chose the streets, we chose everything that comes with it."

"I didn't choose the game; the game chose me! If my father would've——"

"Your father didn't make you choose a life of crime," Deacon Jenkins stated sternly. "You made that decision, not him. That choice was yours for you alone to make. Although we both made the choice to learn life the hard way, I'm going to show you why that choice wasn't in vain. I'm going to help you understand why you're still alive. I'm going to help you see that God has a plan for you."

"Here we go with this bullshit again," I groaned.

"Yeah, that way!" Deacon Jenkins fired back. "Why do you think that you're still alive, Kevin? If what I heard, and what you say, is true, then what makes you so special? People die every day, Kevin. Every. Single. Day. You've got people chasing you around trying to kill you, yet, here you are talking to me."

On the real, I was ready to check the shit outta this nigga. Being nice to these dudes hadn't done nothing but made me more pissed off. Although part of me wanted to set these fools straight, the other half of me wanted to hear what he had to say.

"Okay, look," I finally said. "I don't know why I'm still alive. I just am. If everything you've told me is true, then why are you still here? You claim to have been in similar situations as me. Then how did you survive?"

Deacon Jenkins peered over at Pastor Johnson and smiled. I could tell by the way he was acting that I'd probably asked just the question that he'd been waiting for me to ask.

Chapter 1
The Present
Deacon Jenkins

"I survived because I changed, Kevin. Once God allowed me to experience what I felt, one night, from that moment on he had my undivided attention."

Kevin laughed. "What kind of experience could you have possibly felt that caused you to be scared straight?"

"I didn't say anything about being scared straight. He allowed me to feel something." I shrugged.

"What?"

"I don't know. Something. I can't explain everything that happened to me in only two words. If you'll allow me to, I'll tell you a story."

Kevin peered over at Pastor Johnson skeptically, but gone was the hardened man that he'd portrayed himself to be. The man I saw before me was almost childlike, lost in a state of confusion. What I was about to share with him should help him understand.

"Many years ago, I was just like you. I had no patience for anything outside of what I wanted. My life consisted of the typical things that a person would indulge in when they don't have discipline. Regardless of how entrenched my life was in sin, I still believed in God. My parents were God-fearing people that'd planted such a belief in me as a child. Although, somewhere along the line, I'd stopped worshiping God and became a slave to money, I would always keep the faith that there was a God.

"As I grew older, I became fascinated with the lifestyle of being a drug dealer. It didn't take long before I started selling drugs and doing practically everything under the sun to make some money. As you can imagine, it wasn't long before the haters got involved. Everywhere I went, there was chaos. One night, I was even robbed outside a gambling shack and left face down in the freezing snow, unconscious. Shortly after all that went down, I decided to lay low for a bit. Not only did I need to get myself together, but I needed to allow time to smother hell's flames that were lapping at my feet.

"Around that time in my life, I had a right-hand man named Dirt. Wherever I went, Dirt went. If I went out on a date, Dirt went out on a date. Dirt's sole purpose was to watch my back. I can't front like I paid him tons of money to do the job that he did for me. I simply gave him cheaper prices for the drugs I fronted him than I gave everyone else. That enabled him to give out his drugs on consignment and let someone else worry about selling it.

"Back in those days, I liked to wear a bunch of jewelry. Jewelry was like stink bait to a catfish. The gold diggers flocked to it. Being that I liked to wear a bunch of jewelry, Dirt liked to wear a bunch of jewelry as well. But, Dirt's jewelry wasn't as nice as mine. Dirt wore plain Jane gold rings with no diamonds in them. His chain was a tiny gold rope with no drip to it. Just to keep from outshining my right-hand man, I bought him. a diamond ring and gold necklace that was almost identical to mine. Every day, Dirt shined like new money. His reputation soared because of the added flavor. Every day, Dirt had a different woman on his arm, all courtesy of the new bling I'd bought him. But, for whatever reason, Dirt stopped wearing his jewels. When I asked him why, he told me some lame excuse that ultimately got switched around a thousand different times.

One day, we were in Oklahoma City visiting some lady friends of his. It had been weeks since I'd noticed Dirt stopped wearing his jewelry. So, when we walked in to his new so-called girlfriend's apartment and I saw his chain draped around her neck, I snapped.

"You lettin' random bitches wear your jewelry?"

Dirt looked from me to his new love, embarrassed by my rude outburst. "Come on, Murda J," he said as he ushered me back outside on the front porch. "I told her to hold my stuff since you and me are always in traffic."

Any other time, that excuse might suffice. Any other time, I might not have said another word. Any other time I might have acted like I hadn't seen a thing. But that day wasn't any other time. That day, the weight of the world was bearing down on me.

"Go back inside and get your things so we can go," I told him.

Dirt looked as if he could believe what I'd just said. "But we just got here!" He exclaimed. "I know you're not trippin' because I let my girl wear my chain?"

I didn't have to say another word for him to get the picture. Once I got in my feelings about something, I was a hard young man to deal with. Needless to say, Dirt went and did exactly what I'd told him to. With all the chaos happening in my life, it didn't take much to send me over the edge.

On the ride back to Guthrie, I drove in silence. I couldn't help but think Dirt was starting to act like all the other lying, conniving snakes in my life. Besides the fact that he'd lied about his chain, I suspected that he'd been stealing from me. The last couple of packs I'd fronted him, the money came back short. Never once did I step to him about it. My hustler instincts had kicked in. I knew better than to let my right hand know what the left was doing. I simply kept a close eye on him and now it was time to find out where his loyalty lay.

"I've been meaning to ask you something," I said after I'd parked in my father's driveway back in Guthrie. "The last couple of packs that I've fronted you, the money came back short? I tried to give you the benefit of the doubt that it was a mistake, but then it happened again. Am I trippin'? Or, are you stealing from me?"

Dirt laughed, trying to ease the tension. "You know me better than that," he said. "I'd never bite the hand that feeds me. If the money came back short, I'll take the blame. I'll make it up to you on the next package."

A smiling face in a serious situation was something I'd been taught to never trust. "I'm sure you'll be able to come up with something better than that. You collect your money the same way I do. If the money is short, that means that either you, or someone that works for you, is stealing from me. Now, do you still wanna take the blame?"

Dirt peered over at me solemnly and said, "Relax, big homie. I know it's a lot of fake-ass niggas frontin' like they've got your best interest at heart, but I ain't one of 'em. I wouldn't ever steal from you. I'll get you your money, just trust me."

Opposed to responding to his obvious attempt to pull the wool back over my eyes, I opened the door and got out. Talking to Dirt could be like talking to a child, at times. He didn't get it. Every time he'd bring me my money, I counted it. It was short. Nothing he could say or do that would make me believe he wasn't stealing from me.

"Son, what's wrong?" my father asked upon me walking in his house. I'd left Dirt waiting outside in the car while I ran in to change clothes.

"Nothing," I replied reluctantly. "I got a headache, plus a few other things going on that's got my head spinning."

My father had been reclined in his La-Z-Boy watching television, but quickly sat up. "Jason!" He shouted, stopping me before I left his sight. "I can tell when there's something serious going on with you. Talk to me. What is it?"

Instead of turning this conversation into a long, drawn-out discussion, I just told him the truth. "Dirt, owes me money. I'm trying to figure out how I should handle him. I kinda got the impression that he thinks this is a game. Like, I won't do something to him."

My father woke up my little sister, who was asleep on the sofa. After he'd sent her off to bed, he turned his attention back to me. "I told you to leave that boy alone," he said. "You and his brother used to fight every year on the last day of school. What makes you think you and his little brother can ever be friends?"

I nodded and used the uncomfortable moment of silence as an opportunity to go into my bedroom. Back in those days, I had a small wardrobe practically everywhere I laid my head. Although I lived in Oklahoma City with my girlfriend, Denise, I was rarely at home.

"Where you off to in such a hurry?" my father asked when he walked in my bedroom and noticed that I'd changed clothes.

"I figured I'd go to Langston for a bit. Give myself some space and time to think things through. It's probably best if I put some distance between me and Dirt. If I keep hanging around him, I'm gon' end up hurtin' him."

My father eyed me curiously as I slid on my leather coat. He obviously had something on his mind; probably even was questioning my true intentions for the evening.

After a little while longer of small talk, I said my goodbyes and strolled back outside where I'd left Dirt. Instead of driving out to Langston like I'd told my father, I drove down into the cul-de-sac where my best friend Brent lived. My family had known his since we were kids. On nights that I stayed in town, I spent the night at his house. By no means was Brent's house a nice one. It was more like a trap house. The doors on his place were so old that they could hardly hold the locks in them. The house had so much structural damage that I was surprised that the city hadn't condemned it yet.

After a few gentle taps at Brent's door, he opened up and welcomed us in.

"Wuz good, Murda J?" he said. "You back in town ready to get this thang poppin'?"

I gave him dap and moseyed over to the love seat and sat down. Dirt sat next to me on the sofa while Brent sat in a kitchen chair directly in front of the television.

"You trying to get high?" I asked and pulled off my coat and laid it next to me.

Brent hiked one foot up on the side of the television and said, "You know how we do. If it's that gorilla piss, then fire it up!"

I removed a vial of PCP from my coat and set it on the coffee table. Before I prepared the cigarette to be dipped, I looked at Dirt and said, "Now, what was you saying about my money?"

He looked just about as confused as he did the first time I'd asked him that. "Come on, Murda J," he said. "I told you. I got you. You can trust me."

Brent purposely laughed. He already knew what time it was. I calmly removed a cigarette from the pack and loosened the tobacco.

"Yeah, I recall you telling me something like that. But when you said it earlier, I'm like, do I wanna believe this nigga? Can I trust this guy? I tried to give you the benefit of the doubt, but that shits for the birds. Let me get that chain off you, playa."

Dirt looked perplexed. "My chain?"

I twisted the lid off the vial and dipped the cigarette in it. when the fluid had soaked up half of the stick, I peered over at Brent and said, "This nigga must think I'm fuckin' around."

Brent howled out in laughter, edging the tension on.

"Murda J, you ain't gotta do this. I'll get you your paper. You've gotta trust me."

The fact that he was acting so cowardly only enraged me more. But when he took off the chain and handed it to me, I knew he wasn't the killa he put on to be.

Four solid knocks at the front door startled everyone. We all looked at one another, trying to figure out who could be outside.

"Who is it?" Brent barked.

"It's Dwayne."

Both Dirt and Brent stare at me wide-eyed, waiting for my response. It was my father. "Hold on!" I exclaimed. "I'll be out in a minute." I quickly passed Brent the dipped cigarette and tucked Dirt's chain in my coat pocket as I slid it on. When I walked outside on the porch, my father eyed me sternly.

"Boy, what are you doing in there?" he asked.

I ran a hand over my mouth, trying to hide the smile. I knew he'd heard what I'd done. The double-pane windows in Brent's living room were in bad shape, right along with the rest of the house. One was broken and the other was stuck open year round.

"Nothing. 'Bout to head out to Langston like I told you. What are you doing out here?"

He stepped closer so that only I could hear what he was about to say. "I heard what you did to Dirt. Give that boy back his necklace and come back to the house."

I smirked and looked out in the street. "This my chain. That nigga owes me. If he would've paid me like I told him to, this wouldn't be happening."

My father shook his head in disappointment and said, "Well, now that all that's out the way, you might as well leave. Don't make no sense hangin' around and end up gettin' in trouble. You got his chain, right?"

"Yeah, but I ain't ready to go just yet. I'm fixin' to go holla at them for a while. It'll be an hour or so before I head out to Langston."

My father stepped in my line of sight and said, "That's not gon' cut it. Either, get in your car and leave, or I'm fixing to call the police. It's your choice."

Regardless of whether he was my father or not, if he said something, he meant it. Rather than take a chance of ending up in jail, I decided to leave. I could finish taking anything else I wanted later.

The drive out to Langston gave me plenty of time to reflect on what was happening in my life. I felt like I was losing control. I had one foot in the grave and the other in a bad situation. Every day, something bad was happening. Either I was ducking the cartel, or I had beef with a slew of up and coming rivals. I prayed and asked God not to let my enemies get me. I literally felt death lurking around every corner I came upon. If there was any truth to the saying that God answered prayers, I was looking forward to his response.

Shortly after I arrived in Langston, I was on Langston University's campus in the apartment buildings. Each apartment housed at least three students. The bedrooms had twin beds, and cheap furniture decorated the living room and dining room. The girls lived with the girls and the boys lived with the boys.

By the time I'd found a place to park, I was being scooped out by two girls. My blue convertible Camaro stuck out like a sore thumb. People knew I wasn't from around there.

The two young women greeted me as soon as I got out. Opposed to being messy, I pulled my hood over my head and kept walking. It'd be just my luck that the girl I was there to see looked out and saw me talking to them. I had enough problems as it was. I just wanted to chill.

When I knocked on Crystal's door, I did a quick assessment of my gear. I wore a blue turtleneck Echo sweater with dark denim jeans. My tan Lugz boots matched the gigantic yellow rhinoceros that covered the front of my sweater. My gold chain had a big gold cross that dangled from it. No question, she'd be diggin' my swag.

"It sure took you long enough," Crystal said when she opened the door. "I was starting to think that you wouldn't show."

I gave her a quick embrace and instantly noticed there were several people there that night. Two guys sat at the table playing dominos, while two others looked on from the living room.

"My bad for taking so long," I explained. " I had to make a few more pit stops before I got here."

"What kind of pit stop causes you to be two hours late?" She'd led me over to the sofa so we could get comfortable. The two guys that looked on from the living room, went to join their friends at the dining room table.

"Whatever kind of pit stop it was, I had to do it. Besides, what's the big deal about what took me so long? I'm here now, ain't I?"

Crystal rolled her eyes and hit a joint that her roommate had passed her. While we continued to have small talk, her roommates kept allowing more and more people in.

"Y'all always deep like this?" I asked.

"Um, did someone forget that this was a college campus?"

"Nah, I just didn't expect to be chillin' in a room full of people that I don't know."

"Sounds like you're paranoid."

"It's not that either. I just don't—"

She took me by the hand and led me into her bedroom.

I met Crystal at a gas station. She was buying Zig-Zag papers and I'd just paid for my gas. When I passed by her to leave, that's when she smelt it. I reeked of Indo. We exchanged numbers, and the rest was history. We'd talked by phone every night for the past week. That night was our first time kicking it.

"I've been thinking," she said as she closed the door behind us. "You didn't get here on time. You're paranoid about being around new people and you wouldn't let me hang up your coat when I of-fered. What exactly was it that you do for a living again?"

I plopped down at the foot of the bed while she busied herself in the mirror. The last thing we were about to talk about was what I did for a living. She could think whatever she wanted to about me. Some things a person shouldn't know.

"Whatever I do for a living, you can rest assured it'll never affect you. Let's not let the small things eat away at our time together. This is our first night chillin'. There's a lot more interesting about me than that."

She seemed to ponder that for a moment, yet didn't look away from the mirror. "I see things differently," she said. "If I'm seeing someone, I should have the right to know what type of things he's involved in."

"So we're seeing each other now?" My cell phone rang.

She looked at me through the mirror. "Obviously, you're involved in something. You get phone calls late at night and you wear a bunch of jewelry."

I held up my hand and answered the phone. To my surprise, it was Dirt. He apologized for what he'd done and swore that it'd never happen again. But the more I sat there and listened to him beg for forgiveness, the more I began to doubt his sincerity. I hung up. "Now, where were we?"

Crystal sat at the head of the bed and propped a pillow behind her back. "You were telling me what you do for a living."

"Oh, that part. Why is it so important what I do for a living?"

"Because, I'm in school. I want a nice house. A nice car. Kids. A husband with a phat-ass bank account. What sense does it make to be with someone that doesn't want the same things I want?"

My phone rang. I was surprised that it ran this time. Not many people had my new number. I changed phones frequently to try and stay ahead of my phone being tapped. "Hello?"

"Where are you?" my father asked.

"In Langston, like I told you."

"Sorry to call and make you feel as if I'm trying to be all up in your business, but, the way you were acting earlier had me worried."

I smiled bashfully, knowing Crystal had heard every word he'd said. When I answered the phone, I had put it on speaker phone, but I quickly turned it off.

"Listen, you kinda caught me at a bad time," I told my father. "I'll call you back later, okay?"

"Are you heading back this way tonight?"

"I should be."

"If you decide to come this way, stop by the house. I'd like to see you."

We talked for a little while longer before I finally hung up. By the time I turned my attention back to Crystal, her frustration was evident. "Why are you rockin' your leg like that?" I asked.

She glared at me and snarled, "Because, I'm mad!"

I chuckled. "Don't tell me you're upset because I answered my phone?"

"No, I'm mad because you're not paying attention to me. I brought you in here so we can talk. Not you and—"

My phone rang. "It's not my fault that everybody and their momma need to holla at me."

Crystal got up and tried to walk past me.

"Hold up!" I blocked her exit with my arm. "Where do you think you're going?"

She looked as if I should've already known the answer to that question. "In the living room with my friends," she snapped. "You obviously don't need me in here. I'll just leave you alone so everybody and their mother can talk to you." She attempted to move my arm so I grabbed her wrist.

"Slow down for a second," I said. "I drove all the way down here just to see you. Don't let something you don't understand cause you to act like this."

"I'm not acting like nothing!" she replied sarcastically. "I just think you need some privacy."

My phone stopped ringing. "If you'll sit back down, I've got something to show you."

"Show me what? You can show me whatever you want while I'm standing right here."

"Come on, Crystal. I bought you something. Don't ruin the mood because my phone rang."

Reluctantly, she walked back to the head of the bed and sat back down. For whatever reason, I dug into my coat pocket and pulled out Dirt's chain. I don't know what made me do it. I just did.

"Are you serious?" she asked while staring wide-eyed at the beautiful necklace I held in front of her.

"Why wouldn't I be? Turn around so I can help put this thing on you."

She spun around anxiously, waiting for me to clip the necklace around her neck. When I finally finished, she jumped up to admire herself in the mirror. "This is gorgeous," she said. "It's kind of big to be a woman's necklace, but it still looks good on me. Is this what you do for all the new girls that you start dating?"

"So we're dating now?"

"Maybe."

"The necklace did that?"

She laughed.

My phone rang.

"Here we go again. I wonder who it could be this time?" Crystal eyed me skeptically through the mirror. "Go ahead and answer it," she said ."I suggest you take all the phone calls that you can, 'cause when I'm done taking a shower, I'm going to need some *me* time." She winked.

"Hey, babe." Denise said when I answered the phone. "Where are you?"

I didn't say nothing. I just sat there.

"Babe?"

Nothing.

"Jason!"

"Yeah, that's it. Just put it up there." The phone line fell silent. I was giving my best impression of someone talking to someone else. "Yeah, I'm here."

"What was all that about?" she asked.

"The money in there too."

"What?"

"Let me hit you back."

"Grrrr," she growled. "You get on my nerves. Where are you?"

"I'm telling you, it's all in there."

"I don't even hear no one in the background," Denise hissed. "What are you doing?"

It took everything in me not to laugh. While I held the phone to my ear, acting like I was talking to someone, Crystal had sat back down and was watching me. "Fine! Call me back." I hung up.

My phone rang. What in the hell?

It was Dirt. "Murda J, just hear me out, dawg. I wouldn't never steal from you. You my muthafuckin' nigga! I got luv fo——"

"I ain't trying to hear that shit, right now. You lucky I left when I did."

"I know. I know," he said. " But you had every right in the world to be mad at me. I got $3,500 for you."

"I know you do. You also gon' have the rest of my money too."

"You want me to bring it to you?"

The first thing that came to mind was this was a set-up. I thought back to when me and his brother used to fight all the time. They were not going to catch me slipping that night.

"I want you to leave me the fuck alone," I said. "When I'm ready to talk, I'll let you know."

"I can't believe you actin' like this. Just let me bring you your money. Where you at? Langston? You at some hoe's house?"

"Dirt, I'm telling you. If you come down here, I'ma light yo' shit up. Now, leave me the fuck alone and I'll call you tomorrow."

I hung up.

My phone rang.

I frowned. "Hello?"

"Babe. Where are you?" It was Denise, again.

"Maaannn, I told you that I'd call you back."

"I know you did. I just miss you. When you coming home?"

By now, my frustration had peaked and splintered into what if's. Why did everyone want to know where I was and who I was with? I thought of several different scenarios that would explain what was going on, then I remembered the prayer. This must've been a warning. "I've gotta go," I said and jumped up to leave.

"Why? Is something wrong? Did——"

I grabbed Crystal and kissed her. That was the only thing I could think to do to keep the situation calm.

"I'll tell you about it some other time. I gotta go." I don't know why I was leaving. Maybe I was just spooked. In my mind, that was God's way of telling me I had to get out of there.

I rushed outside into the chilly night air. As I walked through the breezeway, headed to the parking lot, I saw the same two girls that I'd seen earlier. They looked on from the back patio of an apartment upstairs with smiles. By the time I'd made it to my car and looked back, their smiles appeared to be snarls. Even as I stepped closer, they looked more hideous.

Quickly, I got in the car. My hands were trembling so bad I accidentally dropped the keys on the floor. *Calm down*, I told myself. *It's all in your head. You must be high.*

I started the car and noticed that only part of the dash lights were working. The trim around the speedometer was lit up in orange, while the trim around the stereo was lit up in blue. At first, I figured I'd blown a fuse, then I added this strange coincidence with what had just happened. Something was wrong.

I drove back through the campus and onto Highway 33. Highway 33 was a dark two-lane road that connected Guthrie to Langston. An untold number of people had crashed to their doom on the hilly country highway. Slowly, a strange feeling began to form in my chest. This wasn't the type of feeling commonly known as an anxiety attack. This was different. This felt like something was inside of me that wanted to get out!

I drove for a little while longer and exited off the highway onto a dirt road that ran behind an old gas station. I didn't know if the feeling I felt was the first sign of a heart attack or what I felt. I just knew I had to find some place to park. As an added precaution, I turned down another road that led further away from the highway. I couldn't afford for the cops to pass by and see me. I was a well-known drug dealer with a gun in the car. I pulled to the side of the road when I couldn't see anything but pine trees and open fields around me.

It was a full moon that night. I had a clear view of everything around me. The sky was so utterly beautiful I couldn't help but gaze up into it. The stars, the moon…absolutely beautiful.

Suddenly, the temperature in the car felt warm, stuffy. I took off my coat and tossed it on the backseat. *Breathe*, I told myself. But I couldn't. It was hot. I got out.

The cold night air had absolutely no effect on me. I was still burning up. I paced back and forth before taking off my sweater and tossing it in the car as well. Any other time, I wouldn't dare feel comfortable enough to be on a dark country road, alone. But that night, something was different. That night, I felt safe, untouchable, at such a great peace. I feel to my knees and wept. I cried and cried. I cried until my tears of joy turned into praise to God.

"Thank you, Jehovah! Thank you, Jehovah! Thank you, Jehovah!"

A violent quaking sound erupted around me. It sounded as if I was bowing down next to a passing train. But there were no passing trains near that road. The closest train tracks were several miles away. I dug my fingers into the soil, feeling the need to hold on to something. Anything. The world shook. Praise fell from my lips as if they'd been commanded to come forth.

"Thank you, Jehovah! Thank you, Jehovah! Thank you, Jehovah!"

Surely, this was the day my father had told me about: Judgment Day. I had been waiting for this moment. The chance to see his face, The chance to see God.

"Thank you, Jehovah! Thank you, Jehovah! Thank you, Jehovah!

The moon rained down its heavenly glow so bright it seemed to be hovering just above my head. My eyes were transfixed on my gold cross dangling in front of me. Just as I gathered myself enough to look up, it all stopped. No rumbling. No shaking. The moon still shone high above, but darkness had covered the pine trees and open fields. It was just me and darkness.

I stood and swiped away the dirt from my jeans. What happened? Did I really just see that? Unable to think of a reasonable explanation for what I'd just experienced, I got back in the car.

The blue 1991 convertible RS Camaro had a top that folded down inside of a small compartment, between the trunk and the backseat. In order to drop the top, I'd push a button and the back of the top would raise. Then I'd open the small compartment and fold the top down inside of it.

As I drove further down the road, looking for a spot to turn around, I heard the back of my top hitting the latch. I stopped in the middle of the road and spun around to fix the problem, and that's when I came face to face with something.

My coat was propped up in the backseat as if someone was wearing it. The way the moon shone through my small back window gave that something a figure. Its head was facing straight towards me, but I couldn't see any distinguishing features. Part of me wanted to get the hell out of the car and run for dear life, but the other part pleaded for me not to panic. All I kept telling myself was, *Drive, Jason. Drive and don't ever look back. Drive until you make it back to your father's house.* And that's what I did.

I'm sure there was a line of cars behind me as I drove well under the speed limit. I didn't care. I was focused on the road in front of me. The angry drivers with blaring horns were only a distraction, something to make me look back. I was having a hard time trying to understand what was going on in front of me. The signs along the side of the highway weren't in English. They weren't written in any language that I'd ever seen before.

***

Kevin laughed. "Maybe it was written in alien."

I shrugged. "Don't know. Can't say. I do know that Guthrie looked like a totally different city. It looked like a city of gold. Something promising. Then, I didn't understand what I was looking at, but now I do."

"I think I'm starting to understand too. Sounds like you were high and blanked out and started trippin' about God."

"Trippin'— about God?" I smiled. "Tell me. Do you think God talks to us?"

Kevin appeared to think about it. He peered over at Pastor Johnson, who looked on intently.

"Yeah. Kinda."

"Do you pray?"

"Sometimes."

"How?"

"Like everybody else. I close my eyes and say a prayer."

"Do you say it aloud, or silently?"

He scoffed. "Silently. Why?"

"Two things. Now you need to understand just how close your connection is to God. You don't even have to move your lips and he hears you. Next, you are in a relationship with the Creator. Any relationship takes communication. Dreams and visions are a few methods of communication God used in the bible."

"So that's it," Kevin said. "You think God was trying to tell you something?"

I chuckled and stood to leave. "That's exactly what happened. What happened on the dirt road, that was to get my attention. What was in my backseat— that's what would be waiting for me if I ever went back. Back to the streets."

"So you quit hustlin'?"

"I quit— everything. The angry drivers with blaring horns were just what I said they were. A distraction. Something to cause me to look back. Something to cause me to wanna go back. Open your eyes, Kevin. God is trying to tell you something. He talks to us all the time. Some of us just don't recognize his voice."

As Kevin watched the deacon and the pastor leave, he couldn't help but think about what Deacon had told him. *Man, how I wish that was me. I could only imagine what that experience must've felt like.* Whether it happened or not, he believed it did, so it did. Kevin wanted to feel what he felt. Better yet, he wanted a chance to turn around and do right, because God let him know something tragic was about to happen.

Chapter 2
Kevin
15 years ago

The day of O-Dawg's funeral was on a cold and rainy Sunday. The handful of people in attendance were mostly spectators, people that couldn't care less if the homie was dead or alive. With all the low-down things he'd done, it was hard to imagine how many of them had genuine love for him. I can't say anyone loved him more than Ms. O'Dell. We were in for the fight of our lives when they lowered O-Dawg's casket into the grave. If it weren't for several of us, Ms. O'Dell would've gone in after him.

I'm sure that everyone that had love for O-Dawg lost a part of themselves that day. LaShura, wasn't the same snobby bitch I'd been into it with since the night of my birthday party. Surprisingly, she lost the attitude and even asked if I'd spend the night to help lookout for Ms. O'Dell and O-Dawg's little brother. Out of love, for everybody, I did it. I slept on the sofa while everyone else slept in their bedroom. Every night before we went to bed, we held hands and said a prayer for the homie. I think the saddest thing I saw at the funeral was Saira, Cortney's daughter. Saira was like Ms. O'Dell. Sometimes she was there, often she wasn't. Cortney's mother must've prayed long and hard for her the night O-Dawg was murdered. By the grace of God, whoever killed him let Cortney and her daughter live. Cortney was found the next morning, wandering barefoot down a country road. The old white farmer that had found her almost kept driving, but then he noticed the child Cortney was carrying was covered in blood. Whatever Saira saw that night plagued her little mind like a sickness that left her crippled. Occasionally she'd scream, "James!" and then drift off into an uncomfortable silence.

The Logan County Sheriff's Department worked tirelessly until they found where O-Dawg's body was buried. Detectives tried desperately to get Cortney to talk, but she didn't. I don't know if she wouldn't because she couldn't remember, or simply because she didn't want to. But I do know she was terrified. No matter how much I tried to convince her that she was safe, she wouldn't say a word.

I bent over and hugged Cortney tightly. She may have been nothing more than a piece of ass to the homie, but she loved that nigga. In my eyes, that was the common denominator that made us just like family.

"Look, I gotta go," I said while looking down at her with concern. She hadn't budged since the funeral had concluded. While everyone else said their goodbyes and hurried out to their cars to escape the rain, only a few of us still remained.

"You can go ahead and leave," she replied softly. "I'll just be a little while longer. I have a few more things I'd like to say before we leave."

Judging by the people that catered the service, they, too, were ready to leave. Several workers quickly folded chairs while others tided up the burial ground.

"Ms. O'Dell is having a get-together later this evening. You should come through. There'll be plenty of drank, food, and sweets if you want some. Most of the people that'll be there is family, so you're more than welcome."

She nodded as if she was interested, but I could tell she really wasn't.

As I hurried out to my car, I was greeted by an old classmate named Derrick Polk. Derrick was the last person I expected to see at O-Dawg's funeral. Between the two of them, I don't know which one hated the other the most. Our high school teacher, Ms. Green, boasted that Derrick was the most likely to succeed. Although I hadn't seen him in over four years, judging by his appearance, Ms. Green was right.

"Kevin muthafuckin' Dunlap!" he exclaimed jokingly. "What it do, my nigga?"

"It's been a minute since the last time I saw you." The rain had started coming down much harder. I waved for him to follow me.

We dipped between cars, over mud puddles, and finally to where I was parked. Derrick shuffled around to the passenger side and got in.

"This weather is crazy as shit, right?" he said and swiped raindrops from his suit jacket. "One minute it's sunny, the next it look like a tornado is about to hit."

"Pops told me it was going to be like this," I told him. "You know, me being me, I didn't listen. Now, look at me." We laughed, but I noticed he'd taken a good look at the car behind us. "It's probably someone's car that works for the funeral company."

Derrick looked at me quizzically. "The car parked behind us is mine. I just stopped by to check on you. I've been hearing a lot about you. You good? You still holding the hood down?"

The hood had never been a part of conversation. Derrick was a tall lanky nerd, back in high school. Somewhere between then and now, he must've stepped his game up.

"I'ma always hold the block down," I assured him. "Lately, thangs been a little *tuff*, but I'll weather the storm. I'm built for this."

"Maybe a change in occupation might do you some good," he said and handed me his business card. DP's Detail Shop was written across the top in big bold letters.

"What am I supposed to do with this? I hope you don't think I'm tryin' to be wiping down cars. I'm spoiled on this street money. Ain't much a 9-5 can do for me."

He laughed. "Me either! If you're ever interested in trying something different, call me." Headlights flickered on the car behind us. He reached for the door handle.

"It's been someone waiting for you this whole time?"

"When you hunt as a pack, you move as a pack. I'll get up with you later." He got out.

Nothing about Derrick screamed street. He looked like an office executive.

With money already tight and the block at a standstill, I figured, what's the worst that could happen?

***

LaShura

What am I supposed to do now that everything was on me? The food, the bills, time, money…it was all up to me to take care of.

Shouldn't I have time to mourn the loss of my brother? What about my feelings? Does that matter? Do I matter? How was I to know the clicking sound I heard the night my brother was killed was his last cry for help? Detectives told me it was him that had called and I was devastated.

The phone rang.

"Hello?"

Clickety click click click click. Clickety click click click click. Clickety click click click click.

I looked down at the phone, frowning, trying to figure out what in the hell was going on.

"Hello!"

Clickety click click click click. Clickety click click click click. Clickety click click click click.

I hung up.

I expected to hear Stanley begging for my forgiveness. I wanted to tell him how much I loved him, how much I needed him, that I accepted his obvious lies as truth. I wanted to tell him so many things, but instead, I heard the incomprehensible clicking that would haunt me for the rest of my life.

The pastor that spoke at my brother's funeral, likened the consequences of our actions to that of a chisel. He said, "When you're confronted with life's most trying situations, things that challenge your very *will* to exist, know that you're being prepared. It is through these trying times that we acquire some of life's most precious jewels. Wisdom, knowledge, and understanding."

At first, none of his so-called words of wisdom meant anything to me. How I was expected to learn something from such a tragic situation was beyond my understanding. Every day I opened my eyes, my test for the day was how to escape the pain that was hitting me from every angle. My favorite pastime had evolved from lavish shopping sprees to smoking weed with Kevin every day. Whenever I was high, I felt in control. I wasn't hurting. I told myself that I'd quit smoking weed just as soon as the pain wasn't so unbearable. Nobody told me that the pain was here to stay; that the only way to overcome it, was to find a healthy way to deal with it.

In my haste to avoid the loneliness associated with losing some-one I loved, I called on the one person I knew could fill that void. Stanley.

"Why are you standing out here in the freezing cold like this?" he asked.

I was leaning against the wall on my mother's porch when he pulled up. Days had passed since we found out that my brother was dead. Although Stanley had called every day since we broke up, I still hadn't told him what happened.

"I don't know " I finally replied in a nonchalant manner. "I guess I just needed some fresh air. I got a lot coming at me. Stuff that I need to figure out."

Stanley seemed to ponder what I'd just said. He draped his coat over my shoulders and curiously peered inside my mother's house. Luckily, Kevin didn't spend the night that night. He left hours ear-lier after we smoked a blunt and shared a cup of my brother's fa-vorite drink, gin and juice.

"When I spoke with you over the phone, you sounded upset," he went on to say. "Is something else going on, or something you want to talk about?"

I gazed out into the street while anxiously trying to figure out my best approach. How would the police do it? How would they get someone to admit something without making it obvious that's what they were up to? "I was upset, because I don't understand why all of this is happening to me."

"All of what? Toyia? I already told you, she was a mistake. I was just using her to—"

"James is dead."

Stanley looked as if he were having a hard time processing what I'd said. "He's what?"

"Dead."

Stanley stepped closer while his eyes searched mine for the truth. I guess now that we were so close, he could tell something was different about me.

"Are you high?"

I shoved him away and said, "What difference does it make? Don't nobody say nothin' when you come home drunk, high, and talking on the phone to some bitch! I don't need your permission to do anything."

He laughed. "You're grown, that's one thing that you most definitely are, but I'm just saying."

"Instead of trying to figure out whether I'm high or not, shouldn't you be asking me about my brother?"

He sighed heavily. "You're right. What was I thinking? What happened?"

"I already told you, he's dead."

"I understand that, but how did he die?"

I folded my arms across my chest and looked at him as if he should've known the answer. "That's what I was hoping you'd be able to tell me. Where were you the night that my brother was killed?"

Stanley's head snapped back as if I'd spit on him. "That's what this is about? You wanted me to drive all the way down here for this? If it'll help ease your mind, I've been at home every night, hoping you'd walk through the front door. I love you, LaShura. I would never do something like that, especially knowing that it would hurt you."

"Boy, please. Were you thinking about hurting me when you were fuckin' Toyia?"

"That's just it! I wasn't thinking at all. All I was thinking about was——"

"You!" I yelled, completing his sentence the way I felt it should be. "All you think about is you. Everything is about you. You killed my brother because you—"

"Hold on, ma. Don't go throwin' that shit out there like I actually done that."

"Well, if you didn't, then who did?"

He shrugged. "How the fuck am I supposed to know? This is the first time I've heard about this. I got other things going on besides worrying about your brother. He wasn't even on my level."

"Sure coulda fooled me. I distinctly remember the look on your face when James pointed that gun at you. You can act tuff, but I know the truth."

"I didn't drive all the way down here for this," he said. "If arguing is what you called me to do, you shouldn't have even wasted our time." He turned as if he were fixing to walk back to his car.

I snatched him back around by the sleeve of his shirt. "Don't try and walk away from me! You leaving so you can run back to your little girlfriend and tell her everything?"

He looked down at my hand still gripping his shirt. "Let me go."

"Why should I? Are you scared to talk? You ready to leave 'cause you afraid you might slip up and say something?"

He laughed and snatched his arm away from me. "I'm ready to leave before this turns into something it wasn't supposed to be," he snarled. "If you still tryin' to figure out where I was the night your brother was killed, call down to the Sheriff's Department, tomorrow. They should be able to tell you everything I know."

From that moment on, I felt the wedge between us growing deeper. So many questions that deserved answers. So many answers that deserved more questions, but then there'd be more answers and more questions. Before I knew it, I'd be right back at square one again. So many questions that deserved answers.

Daddy told me to be strong and not let none of the foolishness bring me down. He said that although the same foolishness was literally ripping him apart. Between James being killed and the added guilt my mother put on him, my father had changed.

During the days that led up to my brother's funeral, the psychological damage done to my parents became more evident. My mother would start an argument with Daddy for no reason. She blamed him for what happened to James. She blamed him, although he was nowhere near Guthrie the night James was murdered. I tried to reason with her that it wasn't Daddy's fault, to no avail. To try and reason with Momma while she was drunk was like telling a hungry lion not to eat you. She had no understanding.

Most of the time when I tried to talk to Momma, I was just as tipsy as she was. What good was I to try and be the voice of reason? What good was I even to myself? Whenever Daddy came to visit, that was my mother's opportunity to find balance. Outside of the constant nagging and fussing she'd do, she'd often hit him. Never once did he lift a finger to defend himself. He just took it. I imagine he must've blamed himself for what happened to James, just like I blamed myself for not knowing what the clicking meant.

What if my parents had never gotten a divorce? What if Daddy had been there to raise us? I'd asked myself more than 1,008 times. I'd asked myself so many times that I'd lost count. I asked Kevin just to see what he'd say, but that was a mistake. He was too busy trying to be something he wasn't.

What next when the vows are broken? What next when it's left to a woman to raise a man? Was it Daddy's fault?

My best friend, Nikki, always knew the right thing to say when difficult questions arose. The bad thing about that was, I was never able to be that rock for her. Her faith in a Higher Power was the anchor that kept her stable. While I swayed whichever way the wind blew, her faith kept her grounded. Nikki always said Stanley was no good for me, that something about him spelled trouble, that I should be content with my relationship with Darrel. But that was before I caught him cheating, before I busted out his windows, before Nikki got shot, back when I was happy.

POP! POP! POP!

Stanley opened fire, sending people scattering everywhere. I heard car alarms go off. I heard people scream. I heard people yell. I heard cars start. I heard cars speed away. When the dust finally settled, I saw Nikki. She'd been shot.

"Nikki!" I bolted from Stanley's truck over to where she lay face down in the dirt. A puddle of blood oozed from beneath her. Her back twitched as if she was having trouble breathing. I carefully rolled her on her side. "Nikki?"

"Jesus. Jesus. Jesus. Jesus. Jesus," she whispered softly.

"Just breathe. It's gonna be okay. Just breathe."

"Jesus. Jesus. Jesus. Jesus. It hurts."

"I know it does, but hold on. Please." Her breathing slowed to a stop as blood trickled out the corner of her mouth. *"Someone heeelp! She's dying!"*

Nikki's everything was her Lord and Savior. Her faith was in her Lord and Savior. Her strength was in her Lord and Savior. When it was all said and done, she'd dedicated her life to her Lord and Savior. As much as I'd heard about this all-powerful God she served, I looked forward to seeing him do something. Forget what they taught me in Sunday school. Damn what the pastor said. I needed him to do something now.

And He did.

"Move!" a man barked as he shouldered his way through the crowd. It was the guy from inside the club, the one Nikki had danced with. Several of his fraternity brothers followed behind. All of them were dressed in purple. And all of them were there to get Nikki. *"How bad is it?"* He asked.

I looked down at her. *"It's bad. She stopped breathing."*

The man lifted her off the ground as if she weighed nothing. I tried to follow them as he carried her away, but his fraternity brothers wouldn't budge from the wall they'd formed around the car they put Nikki in. When I saw them pull out of the parking lot, a piece of me went with them. Never in my wildest dreams did I think I'd see my friend again. Too much blood. Too far of a drive to the nearest hospital, and I knew damn well the car they drove away in wasn't a fast one.

I told myself, if she lived, I would become a believer. I would tell everyone I knew about what God had done for Nikki. I'd go to church, sing in a choir, and stop cussing. I made 1,008 different promises only to find out...

She lived.

Nikki spent months in the hospital fighting to recover. The bullet from Stanley's gun had nearly cost her her life. Doctors said that she would never walk again. They said because of the damage done to her spine, she'd be lucky to even move her legs. While I cried like it was the end of the world for me, Nikki took his assessment as if it were wishful thinking on his behalf.

"God didn't bring me through this so that you wouldn't believe," she had told me. "He did it so that you would."

To hear someone say that while lying in a hospital bed, tubes running every which way, machines beeping high and low…you can only wish the best for them. You can only try and be optimistic, yet content that that person is still alive. But, when you hear someone say that and witness the fight, applied with faith and miraculously that person overcomes the unthinkable…that'll have an effect on you. It did to me. It made me question who I am in the greater scheme of things.

Every day I was at Nikki's bedside. Every day I was there to wipe away her tears, to see her look defeat in the eye and say, "I'm not done yet." I heard the prayers. I saw the fight. I witnessed what it meant to stand on faith.

Now I understood the chisel.

"Really?" Nikki snapped when she walked in my bedroom and coughed at the smell of smoke. "I hope you don't think I'm fixin' to just stand by and watch you do this to yourself."

I sighed and snipped out the rest of my joint in a Coke bottle top. This was the side of Nikki there was no getting used to.

"Don't start. I'm in here minding my own business. I don't need you, or anyone else, coming in here messing up my mood."

Nikki hobbled around my bed and sat down next to me. The pain I saw etched on her face prompted me to ask, "Are you okay?"

She gently massaged her lower back.

"Yeah. It's just when it gets cold outside, my muscles tighten up. The added tension puts pressure on the bullet, which puts pressure on my spine."

"You think if I run some warm water that'll help your muscles to relax?"

She shook her head. "Let's not make it about me. I'm worried about you."

"There's nothing to be worried about. I'm fine."

"Are you? 'Cause, I hardly call *fine* getting high in a room all by yourself after a funeral. That sounds more like depression. Besides, when did you start smoking weed?"

"See. There you go."

"What?"

"I told you not to start, Nikki."

"This is what people do when they care. I don't see the point in resorting to drugs because you're hurting and don't understand what's happening."

I got up and went to run warm water on a washcloth. Nikki knew exactly what to say that would blow my high. She said the same type of things if I was drunk. "Let me put this on your back." I walked back into the bedroom with the warm towel. I sat on the bed behind Nikki and lifted her blouse. "Does it hurt?" I applied a little pressure with the towel.

"Not really," she replied. "This would work a lot better if the towel was hotter. You can't just use water from the sink and expect for it to do the trick. The water has to be super-hot, almost boiling."

I rolled my eyes and kept dabbing. Warm water from the sink would have to do. I didn't feel like dealing with the sea of friends and family that were crammed in our house. In my opinion, this was the perfect opportunity to do *me*. The last thing I felt like dealing with was being scrutinized by someone else.

"Where's Vance? I'm sure if you're in here, then he's not too far away."

Nikki blushed and tried to hide her smile. Vance was her husband. He'd been by her side since their first dance, back in college.

"Vance is in the living room," she finally replied. "I told him to wait there while you and I could talk."

At the mention of the word talk, I was on my feet headed back to the bathroom. If she wanted to talk, we had a house full of people she could do it with. I just wanted some time to do me."

"I know what you're doing." Nikki said. "You're avoiding me. You're avoiding me because you don't want to hear what I've got to say."

I laughed. "I don't. I'm doing me, right now. I don't wanna hear about what people think I should be doing, or what I should be doing. All I want to think about is whatever I wanna think about. That's what doin' me, means."

"But—"

"There's no buts, Nikki. It's that simple." I shut off the water and peered back into my bedroom. I need to figure out how I was gonna work my way through this. Between the bills, food, my mother…

"That's exactly what I'm talking about. You have a bunch of extra pressure

weighing on you. That's why you've started smoking weed. Your knees are buckling under pressure."

"So what am I supposed to do? I can't simply block all this out. This stuff is happening."

"You've got to remove yourself from the situation."

I was slightly confused. "Are you talking about this situation with my brother?"

She nodded.

"That, and your relationship with Stanley."

"Stanley and I broke up!"

"I know, but you still love him. And as long as you feel that way for him, then you'll always feel attached to him."

"I can't just flip a switch and stop loving him, Nikki."

She hobbled into the bathroom and stood next to me. "I don't expect you to," she said. "This is about removing yourself from the situation."

"And just how do you suggest that I do that?"

"By moving in with us for a while. You've been stuck doing the same routine for a while. It's time to try something different. Maybe you'll have a different outcome."

"I can't just up and leave Momma like that. She needs me."

"No! You need you right now. Besides, it'll be fun. Vance and I are like old people sittin' in the house doin' nothing. I know you like to spice things up a bit. Plus, I can keep an eye on you."

Chapter 3
Kevin
15 years ago

The day after O-Dawg's funeral, Stutter and I went to see DP. Although Stutter was strongly against the idea of possibly working for our classmate, I was still able to convince him otherwise. I was on the brink of going broke. If I was broke, he was broke. He didn't have a plug to get no work and I didn't either.

"Y-you sure that this the place?" Stutter asked as I pulled into DP's shop's parking lot.

I double-checked the address on the card DP had given me. The shop didn't look anything like I'd expected for it to. It looked like a storage unit company had been converted into a detail shop, except the detail shop still looked like a storage unit company. There were no other cars in sight. No people. No signs of business. No nothing. Nothing that might imply that this was a business that specializes in cleaning cars.

"Yup, this is it," I finally replied.

On both sides of the street were several rows of storage units. In the middle of the block was the main office, which was where I'd parked. There was a seven-foot chain link fence that surrounded the units on both sides of the street. An older, bald-headed man watched us through the front window. He eyed us with so much suspicion, I figured it'd be best if we went in.

"Is there something I can do for you gentlemen?" the man greeted us as we approached the counter.

"We're here to see Derrick Polk. I talked to him earlier and told him I'd stop by."

The man scratched his chin and frowned. "You talkin' 'bout DP?"

I laughed. "My bad. I forgot. I'm so used to callin' him by his name."

The man laughed and said, "I know. I was just giving you a hard time. If you give me a sec, I'll call DP and let him know that you're here."

I sat in one of the chairs against the wall while Stutter browsed through the shop's merchandise. Racks upon racks of miscellaneous car accessories were scattered around the room. Strangely, everything looked dusty, like it hadn't been moved in a while. Just as my curiosity piqued and I got up to have a closer look, the man hung up the phone.

"A'ight fellas, just go through this door, hang a right, and you'll see him chillin' in the lounge area."

Stutter and I went through a door that led into the garage. Now I understood why I hadn't seen any cars out front. DP's car was parked in the garage. A vacuum cleaner sat next to it and a long red water hose stretched across the garage floor.

"Hell must've froze over if you're here," DP said jokingly. "I thought you was bullshitin' when you said you was comin' through."

I looked around the lounge area. A floor model television sat in the corner and four office chairs were positioned around it. "A nigga too broke not to stop by and at least find out what you've got going on."

DP nodded in agreement then gestured for us to have a seat. "I used to be just like you. Always on the come-up, always broke, always trying to figure out what my next best move should be." He shook his head. "That shit is over with. Once Short blessed my game, I haven't looked back since."

"Who in the hell is Short?"

"The ole head you met when you first came in."

"Oh, that's Short. I can see why they call him Short. He also talk funny, like he ain't from around here."

He chuckled. "Short is from my hometown back in Mississippi. He moved down here to help out around the shop. His level of expertise was exactly what I needed." DP picked up the remote to the television and hit power. After channel surfing, he landed on BET. "Y'all niggas thirsty? I got cold sodas in the fridge."

Stutter instantly declined the offer, but I was thirsty. "Let me get a Coke."

While DP hurried off to grab my drink, Stutter leaned in so no one would overhear us. "Where's all the customers?" he asked. "Where's any-any-anything at? I don't know what made you think he was gettin' money. Just 'cause he drives a BMW don't mean h-he can afford to."

The door that led into the office opened and DP strolled back in, carrying two drinks. "Sorry I couldn't get you nothing cold to drink," he said. "The refrigerator just went out. I still brought you a Coke just in case you still wanted it."

Stutter gave me a look that said it all.

"Do y'all get much business around here?"

DP shrugged and sat down next to me. "Guess you could say we get enough. I got a shop. My rent is paid for, car paid for."

"Sounds like you're doing good. You makin' it. I thought it'd be hard to attract any customers since ain't nothing but storage units around. The only way someone could stumble across this place was if they needed a storage unit."

DP bobbed his head to the music video on TV. He seemed unconcerned with what I was getting at. Just because he was making money, didn't mean we would be making money.

"I like it that there are no other business around," he finally said. "The less people around, the less traffic. The less traffic, the better chance I have of staying in business."

"But if there's no people around, then how you gon' make money?"

He laughed. "You should know me better than that, Kev. I'm smarter than your average bear. I ain't in the business of cleaning cars. I'm in the business of emptying safes. This shop gives me a legitimate explanation of how I make my rent money, why I have a bank account, and how I'm able to build credit. The list goes on."

"What do you mean by emptying out safes?"

"I mean, walk up in somebody's spot and lay everybody down. By any means necessary. That's the code we live by."

"You ni-ni-niggas hittin' banks and shit?" Stutter asked.

"We hittin' whatever our inside man tells us to. If he puts us on a jewelry story, then that's where we go. If he puts us on a kingpin, then that's who we rob. Our inside man knows how to get us in and out with no problems."

"This like some 007 shit," I said as I nudged Stutter playfully. We got codes and inside men. Next, he'll be pulling out some secret gadgets."

"H-how m-m-much money y'all make off doin' this?" Stutter asked.

"Depends. If I got a crew of two or three, we'll be lucky to get 15 G's. But if I got a crew of five or betta, we'll see anywhere from 80 to a hunnit grand easily."

Stutter and I howled with excitement. But with so much money on the line, why did I have a strange feeling he wasn't telling me something?

"If you've been making that type of money, where's the dudes that helped? Why they ain't around?"

"My niggas is doin' twenty year bids at Leavenworth. We got sloppy, spent money recklessly, put too many people in our business. Before I knew it, the feds were serving indictments. Had I have known what I know now, I'd have done things differently."

The door leading into the front office opened and Short walked in. Nothing about him screamed any level of expertise. He looked like the typical country nigga, if you were to ask me. He wore blue jeans, square-toed boots and a big belt buckle. He looked to be every bit of 50. I say that because of the speckles of gray hair in his beard.

"Dem people wanna know if we're good to go on that issue we discussed," Short said. "This is the second time he's called in an hour. You want me to tell 'em we're in or not?"

DP fumbled with the remote to the television and tossed it on the table. He looked me dead in the eye, then eyed Stutter. "Are you niggas tryin' to make some money, or not?" He asked. "This is the perfect opportunity for y'all to get on. The job ain't too small, ain't too much work involved, and it's a nice price tag attached to it."

"Wh-wh-what is a nice price tag?" Stutter stammered.

"No less than 10,000. The money will get split five ways, though."

"Five ways? I thought it was just gon' be you, me, Short and Stutter. Who else is coming?"

"The fifth person is our inside man. It's only right that he gets a fair share. His job is to give us the layout. By the time I get things back to the way they were, there'll be six of us."

"The bigger the crew, the bigger the job," Short said matter-of-factly. "The bigger the job, the more money. The more money—the more problems. Know that if you step into this lifestyle, it comes at a hefty price."

10,000 dollars was a lot of money to make in one night. Up until that day, I'd never so much as seen that much money. I'm sure Cabbage and his crew was touching that kind of paper, but not me. Not us. We were still bleeding the block flipping rocks. Not only would this give us a chance to elevate our game, but Ms. O'Dell could sure use some help.

Adrian Dulan

Chapter 4
Kevin

For the rest of the day, we went over details about the job we were about to do. By nightfall my excitement to rob someone and make $10,000 had turned into nervousness. I was surprised no one noticed. Everyone seemed to be oblivious to the possible dangers ahead. Short rode shotgun and bobbed his head to the music while DP drove. Stutter sat next to me in the backseat. He stared out the window in a daze, thinking about God only knows what.

The person we were about to rob was a white man named Bill. Bill owned a pawn shop on the eastside of Oklahoma City. He was a well-known gambler that had plenty of money. That revelation alone was enough to let me know he was strapped. I thought someone else might care, but they didn't. The best advice DP had for me was play your part. Everything else, let him worry about.

Since Bill had a wild gambling habit, our inside man, Fifty, was able to track him like clockwork. Friday nights were his table nights. He played poker with his retired military friends, bankers, lawyers, and other business owners. Although everyone that attended poker night had long money, they never gambled high stakes.

Saturday night was an all-out ball until you fall festival. Bill would go from gambling at the horse track to placing bets on cars at the race strip. By the end of the night, he'd generally end up at a dog fight with thousands of dollars on the line. Bill was good at what he did. He was also smart enough to keep his dirty money separate from his legit money. His style of hustle was one that I admired.

Sunday night was Bill's alter ego night. After six days of hustling at every turn, on the seventh, one would think he rested, but he didn't. He turned into a trick. Bill would pick up two of his favorite call girls and duck off to his mini-mansion on the county line.

The Oklahoma County Line began at Waterloo Road. You could exit on to Waterloo Road off of I-35, which was the same highway we used to go back and forth to from Guthrie to Oklahoma

City. Waterloo Road was also where Logan County began. In a nutshell, Bill's player's mansion was on the outskirts of Guthrie. On either side of the highway were heavily wooded areas. Country.

We exited the highway.

"Kev, you and Stutter sit tight while I run and pay for the gas," DP said. "Short, check the oil, but take your time with it. We need to be here long as possible without looking suspicious, without being seen. And all that has to be done while we're on the lookout for Bill. This is normally about the time when he's headed home."

While DP ran inside the gas station, me and Stutter scoped out the parking lot. The Love's gas station was crowded with people, some there to purchase snacks and food, others for gas, or simply a break from the highway. Love's was the perfect spot to spot Bill's big dually truck when it got off the highway. Although a lot of people drove trucks in Guthrie, none of them were quite like Bill's. Bill's was one of a kind. Special Edition. He had stacks behind the cab of his truck as if it were a diesel.

Short opened the passenger door and got back in. He casually flipped down the sun visor and peered through the mirror. "That's him behind us," he said. "It's only three of 'em. Should be quick and easy. In and out."

Luckily, the Grand Marques we were in had tinted windows. I'm sure at some point they'd want to know if they were followed.

"So what now?" I asked. "We can't just sit here and wait for them to leave. That would be a dead giveaway."

DP got back in and slammed the door. He started to say something, but must've noticed the it's not happening look on my face. "You niggas ready?" he asked.

"Hell naw! It's cameras everywhere."

DP scoffed and started the car. "You're nervous," he said. "You done forgot everything I told you. We handle our business the right way. No mishaps. No sloppy movements. Focus."

We rode a little further down the road, mostly without talking. The silence inside the car was deafening. Occasionally, DP would ramble off instructions about what he wanted us to do. Since Short was an electrician, his job was to kill the power while DP got us in.

Stutter and I were given the honors of holding everyone at gunpoint. The mission sounded like a piece of cake. Once the alarm was disabled, we'd have a few minutes to get in and get out before someone showed up.

Up ahead was a large clearing in the dark wooded area. A small cluster of houses came into view surrounded by a split log fence. There was a man-made pond attached to the backyard of all the houses. A circle of lights was in the middle with water spouting from it. Each home had numerous garage doors. Some of the garage buildings were detached from the house, while others were a part of the beautifully-built homes.

"That's where Bill lives," DP said. "I'll find us a place to park and we'll chill for a bit. We gotta give them a chance to get comfortable before we move in."

Instantly, my stomach started churning, bubbling. I was thinking all kinds of weird shit. What if we get caught? What if somebody gets hurt? What if he pulls out a gun? So many thoughts. So many questions. So many reasons why I should have told DP to call it off— but I didn't.

We got out and jogged along the side of the road at a steady pace. The unfamiliar terrain was difficult to maneuver through. The side of the road was lined with tall weeds and a ditch deep enough that we could hide in if need be. When we'd finally reached the split log fence, we hoisted each other over, careful not to hurt ourselves. Judging by the hollow wooden structures and construction equipment scattered about, the small cluster of homes was the beginning of what would become a prestigious community.

The first house, obviously everyone was asleep. No lights were on; only the porch light. The second house startled us all. A motion sensor light popped on as we moved past. Fortunately, the next house was where we were headed.

Bill's massive five-bedroom house stood before us. To our advantage, there was no privacy fence around any of the backyards. That gave us easy access to the back of the house. The backyard looked like something you would see on *MTV Cribs*. Bill had an outdoor fireplace, patio furniture, and hot tub, and smoke seeped from the chimney.

DP pointed up at a light on the corner of the house. That was Short's cue to kill the power. The clock started now. We had ten minutes after the power was cut to get in and get out.

"Wait!" DP hissed. Short stopped. DP pointed towards the patio door. It was open. From inside came the howl of laughter, and country music blared from the stereo. We had a clear view of the spacious living room. Most of the wall around the patio door was made of glass. We inched closer.

Two women were in the living room on the sofa. Bill stood at an island in the kitchen, preparing food for the grill. DP gave us the signal. It was time.

Stutter and I removed the guns DP had given us from under our jackets. Just when one of the women stood and began swirling her hips to the music, we rushed inside.

"Everyone down!" DP shouted. "Get the fuck on the floor, now!"

The woman that had been dancing screamed. I shoved her down on the sofa, so her friend followed suit.

"Whoa, whoaaa, whoaaaaa!" Bill exclaimed, slightly startled. "What's this about?"

Stutter moved swiftly through the living room to the kitchen to where Bill stood. He held his gun inches from his face. "Get. down."

Reluctantly, Bill did as he was told. He kneeled and locked his fingers behind his head. "There's nothing here," he said. "You're wasting your time if you think you'll find anything here."

Short and DP quickly disappeared upstairs. Bill glared up at Stutter, openly expressing his hatred. His nonchalant attitude gave me the impression that there was something there. Had to be.

Moments later, DP ran back down stairs empty-handed. "Where is it?" he barked. His eyes roamed around the room as if he was in search of something.

Bill smirked. "Told you. There's nothing here. I have some credit cards in my wallet. You're more than welcome to 'em if you'd like. Cops will probably be here any minute. No tellin' how many people heard that girl scream."

Stutter must've didn't like what he'd heard. He anxiously rocked back and forth on his heels. "Ain't-ain't none of this stuff worth dying for," he said. "Y-you heard him. Where is it?"

Bill chuckled. "Even if I did have something, I wouldn't give it to—"

BOOM!

The blast sent Bill crumbling to the floor, where he howled out in pain. "My arm! You shot me in the fuckin' arm."

One by one, each of the women began to whimper. Fuck it. My eyes teared up too. That shit wasn't supposed to happen. I didn't want to go to jail.

"I'm going to ask-ask y-y-you one more time," Stutter said with no emotion. "Where is it?"

Bill rolled about on the floor, clutching his arm. To mock Stutter again would surely cost him his life. "It's behind the picture on the wall," he groaned.

We all looked around the living room. Portraits and paintings hung everywhere.

"Which one?" DP snapped.

Bill growled. Spittle bubbled between his teeth as he tried to speak. "The——one—with the Native woman." He pointed over by the book shelf.

Short quickly crossed the room and took the picture down. A six-digit combination and key was needed to get inside the safe.

Stutter put the barrel of his gun on Bill's forehead. "You know-know what we need."

Bill removed his key chain from his belt. "Take it," he said. "Combination is 9-34-26."

Stutter snatched the keys out of his hands and tossed them to Short. Short had the door open in the blink of an eye. Several files sat in plain view along with a black velvet bag. Short took the bag and left everything else.

While Short and DP got a head start back to the car, I noticed Bill had stopped moving. He'd lost a lot of blood. Judging by how pale he was, he was dead.

Stutter dug in his pocket.

"The fuck are you doing?"

Stutter snatched Bill's wallet out of his back pocket and broke the chain attached to it. He then went and emptied the contents of the women's purses on the sofa and took their money as well.

"Stutter, leave that shit alone and let's—" Fuck! I'd said it. His name. I'd said it. Although we both wore masks, I still knew the look of disbelief was etched on his face. Without warning, he pointed his gun at the back of a woman's head.

"Wait!" she screamed.

Pop!

He shot her.

The other woman tried to get up.

Pop! Pop!

He shot her too. He quickly made his way back over to Bill's motionless body and filled him up with bullets too.

Pop! Pop! Pop!

"N-n-now let's-let's go."

Chapter 5
Kevin
The Present

Weeks had passed and I still lay here wondering how I ended up in this situation. The hardest part about trying to make sense of the madness is how easy it is to get stuck dwelling on a bad time in your life. Like the night I was shot and ended up in the stream. Just the thought of that night sent chills down my spine. The darkness I felt at the bottom of that stream was unlike anything I'd ever felt. I clawed at the impenetrable darkness, hoping to fight my way back to the surface. Just as the idea of being hopelessly lost surfaced in my mind, I was found. My feet dragged along the bottom of the stream just as I was suddenly whisked away again. Spinning. Spinning. Spinning. Head over heel, twisting and turning deeper into darkness.

Memories of my daughter awakening me washed over me like a tidal wave. She wore her favorite pink dress with shiny black slippers. "Daddy?"

That's who I was to her. Daddy. That's who I'd always be to her. Daddy. A lot of things I did to ensure that we lived comfortably was wrong. Although I can't say I would've done anything different if given the opportunity, I'd like to think I would.

My father had some choice words for me when he noticed how reckless I'd become. I was at home, in my bedroom, when he walked in and saw what I was doing.

"Kevin, what in God's name has gotten into you?" he asked.

I had just finished bagging up several pounds of ice. Drug paraphernalia lay scattered around the room. As soon as I realized he'd barged in unexpectedly, I tried to put everything away.

"And hello to you too!" I exclaimed in a vain attempt to lighten his mood. "I didn't expect to see you today. Had I known you were on your way, I would've cleaned up a little."

December howled in laughter while she watched her favorite cartoon in the living room. My father closed the door behind himself and strolled over to my bed and sat down.

"What's gotten into that head of yours?" he said. "You used to be much sharper than this, Kevin. You're not using your head. Where do you think the wolves are coming to feast when they find out where their next meal could be?"

I laughed. Niggas knew what it was gon' be if they ever stepped to me like that. "Everythang is cool. I got this. Aren't you the one that always said, my house, my rules? That used to be your favorite line."

He scoffed. "I mighta said that a time or two, but you ain't neva saw me carryin' on the way you are now. People that move like you do are beggin' for something bad to happen to them."

I walked over to the closet and grabbed my heat. Pops would get to rambling on and on about some shit he learned off TV. I had niggas from out of state in town to buy my work. Although I'd never intentionally disrespect my father, since he walked in unannounced, I had to finish getting ready.

"What's that for?" My father asked, while I tucked my gun under my shirt.

"Might need a little protection while I'm out there checkin' a bag. I gotta do what's necessary for the kid to make it back home."

"Looks to me, you done made it back home. You just forgot where you were. You've got a nice home with a beautiful family. And from the looks of all that junk I saw you stuffing in those bags— I'd say you've got a nice chunk of cash somewhere. Don't make no sense to keep rolling the dice when you're winning. Sooner or later, you're gonna miss your point."

"Why you can't just be happy for me? Why you gotta come around messin' up the vibe with all this negative energy? Things are looking good for me. Just 'cause you see something bad don't mean it's all bad. Why don't you start looking at and speaking on the good that I do?"

"I thought that's what I was doin'."

"When?"

"When I said you have a nice home with a beautiful family."

"That's your big compliment?"

"That's what it is, ain't it?" he said snidely. "Lotta boys in them streets don't got what you've got. They might got a nice house, but no one to share it with. Or, a beautiful family, but can't afford a nice place to live. But to have a nice home, a nice chunk of change, and someone to share it with, I'd say you've reached your mark. Don't ever lose sight of why you started hustling. Before you know it, you'll be done missed your mark and lost everything."

I snatched up my Louie bag, hoping he'd catch my drift. Pops had a way of playing on my conscious to try and get his way. When I was younger, that stuff may have worked. Now that I was grown, I had to get to the money!

I headed for the door, but my father jumped in front of me. "There's nothing at the end of that road you're on."

"I know. There. I admitted that I know nothing's at the end of the road. Now can I go? I gotta do something."

He sighed and shook his head. "Haven't you ever wondered where the rest of your family is? Have you ever stopped to think about why your mother and I get a divorce? Doesn't it seem strange that you don't know your family's history?" He stepped to the side so as to allow me to leave. "Stay and I'll tell you everything. Leave, and I guess we'll talk some other time."

Why I didn't stay was eating me alive right now. Every question he'd asked, I needed to know. Maybe that would've shed some light on why things were the way they were.

Chapter 6
Stutter
15 years ago

"Tell him!" Leonard shouted. "Why don't you tell him what kind of a no good, poor excuse of a mother you really are."

I listened from my bedroom as my parents fussed and fought. Ironically, their fighting had become the melody I fell asleep to at night. It was also the same song I awoke to each morning. Listening to them fight didn't bother me as much as it used to. I'd grown immune to it. Whatever secrets they'd been at odds over, they'd been fighting about since I was born. Naturally, I wanted to know what those secrets were, but to ask the wrong question might unleash something in Leonard I wasn't ready to deal with.

"I'll tell him," my mother cried. "Just not now. I don't know when. Just not now."

"When?" Leonard snarled. "You've been tellin' me that same bullshit for years. The boy grown. He need to know the truth."

"I need time. Maybe when he's—"

The thunderous rumbling from their fighting caused the window panes to rattle. I covered my head with a pillow trying to blot out my mother's screams.

Think about something else. Think about money. How much money? A lot of money. Think about——

Boom! Boom! Boom!

The more I tried to focus on something different, the more messed up stuff I thought about.

Boom! Boom!

More fights.

Boom! Boom! Boom!

Murder.

All the screaming and thunderous rumbling made me think back to the last time I saw O-Dawg.

Every time Saira ran through the living room, she caused the CD to skip.

Boom! Boom! Boom! Boom! Boom!

"Saira, stop running in this muthafuckin' house!" O-Dawg barked.

I can't explain the way I felt the moment I saw that nigga's face. Just to hear the sound of his voice put me in another state of mind.

"Back up!" Leonard hissed. "If you get too close to the window, he might see you." No soon as those words had left his mouth, O-Dawg peered in our direction. If it weren't for the cosmetics that lined the inside of the window ledge, I'm certain he would've seen us.

Quickly, we made our way back to the front yard, careful not to make a sound. For the most part, all the neighbors seemed to be asleep. Across the street, a man walked out to his truck and got in. A woman rushed out on the porch behind him. They talked for a bit. The truck started. The man drove away.

Cautiously, we crept up on Cortney's porch and peered through the window.

Saira was in her bedroom having an all-out argument with absolutely no one. You'd think by the way she was acting that she was talking to someone, but she wasn't.

Leonard cocked the hammer back on his gun and knocked on the door. I slid to one side while he stood on the other.

"Who is it?" Cortney shouted over the music.

The sound of her footsteps drew near to the door, sending my heartbeat racing. I gripped the handle of an eight-inch butcher knife as if my life depended on it. Sure, we knew O-Dawg was strapped, but he didn't stand a chance for what we had in store for him.

As soon as the front door started to open, Leonard kicked it in.

Cortney screamed. Leonard rushed in and grabbed a fist full of her shirt. "Get your fucking hands off me!"

They tussled for a moment until Leonard finally got her under control. He pressed that bitch to the side of her head just as Saira ran into the living room.

Boom! Boom! Boom! Boom! Boom!

"Mommy!"

"Hurry up and grab that li'l bitch and shut her fuckin' mouth."

I tried to grab her as she shot past, but she was fast. Real fast. She took off running down the hall.

"James!"

Boom! Boom! Boom! Boom! Boom!

No matter how badly I hated O-Dawg, I knew better than to underestimate him. If given the opportunity, he'd shoot first and ask questions last. When Saira ran into the bathroom screaming his name, I knew she knew where he was hiding. Despite all the noise we made, not once had he shown his face.

I hit the light switch.

"Just the muthafucka that I've been looking for," I snarled. "Pu-pu-put the little girl down so we can finish this."

O-Dawg stood next to the bathtub holding Saira. His eyes shifted from me to her as if somehow, she could save him.

"Finish what?" he replied. "Me and you straight. We ain't eva had no problem."

I marched right up to his face so he could look me in the eye. I wasn't there to play no games or do any talking.

Whop!

O-Dawg went stumbling backwards and fell in the bathtub. He scrambled to get back to his feet, but I was already on him. Wherever the knife landed, he shrieked in pain. Hand, arm, shoulder.

"Ahhh! Shit! Fuck!"

Hip, leg, thigh.

"Heeelp!"

Saira had sense enough to get out of Dodge. The raw adrenaline pumping through my veins had me seeing red. I probably would've got her too if this nigga wasn't putting up such a fight.

"The fuck is wrong wit' you?" O-Dawg panted. He held my wrist, stopping me from hittin' him in the stomach. "If this 'bout money, you can have all dat shit. Just take it and go."

"You think this 'bout money, don't you? You think ev-ev-everything is 'bout money, don't you?" I tilted the blade and sliced his arm.

"Ahhhhh!"

I tried to snatch him out the tub by the pants leg. "Get up!" I yanked and pulled, pulled and yanked. I hit him with the knife a few more times. He refused to die. He was leaking like a stuck pig. All those times he'd made a mockery of me, all those times he'd laughed at my family, all those times he'd fucked my momma for some dope...he was 'bout to die for that shit. I cocked back to commence stabbing and Leonard grabbed my arm.

"Save some for me," he said. "You look out for these two while I even the score with him." Leonard handed me his gun.

"L, I thought we was betta than that," O-Dawg pleaded. "You can have every dime I got to my name."

Leonard took hold of his shirt and lifted him to his feet. They both stared eye to eye before Leonard finally spoke.

"I thought you already understood that we're not here only because of your money."

O-Dawg looked back and forth between me and Leonard. "I got plenty of work too!" He said. "You can have all th——"

"This ain't about no money, no dope."

"Then what's this about? Just tell me. Gimme a chance to fix this. I can make this right."

"How you gon' make it right, and you've been fuckin' my wife?"

O-Dawg stiffened. He knew he was in deep shit. Opposed to prolonging the inevitable, he swung. Leonard ate it and dismantled him with no problem. He was a beast with his hands. When he body slammed O-Dawg on the side of the bathtub, I thought he was dead.

"Drag this muthafucka to the living room!" Leonard ordered. I could hear in his voice he was tired, but that nigga wasn't dead.

I grabbed him by the pants leg and started pulling.

"Bitch, you too!" Leonard snapped at Cortney.

She grabbed O-Dawg's other pants leg and started pulling. By the time we dragged him all the way to the living room, I was pulling, Cortney was pulling, and Saira was pushing. We made it.

"What y-you want me t-to do with her?" I asked about Saira. "Y-you want me t-to tie her up too?"

Leonard seemingly thought about it as he tied up Cortney. "Fuck her," he said. "She shouldn't be too much of a problem. I'll pull the car around front while you make sure these bitches stay put." Leonard peeked out the curtain checking to see if the coast was clear. When he was certain no one was watching, he disappeared out the front door.

"You don't have to do this," Cortney cried. "I have money. Lot' of it. I can write you a check. Just let us leave."

I don't know who she thought I was. If it weren't for Leonard, they'd have been dead. The only one that stood a chance of walking away from this alive was Saira.

"Let's hurry and get them outside to the car," Leonard said upon his return. "We'll put the girl in the front with us and lock them up in the trunk."

Cortney cried. I led her out to the car first and locked her in the trunk. Next, I buckled Saira in the front seat before helping to carry O-Dawg out. The sight of all the blood smeared across the floor didn't bother me, but when we carried O-Dawg outside, I could see steam seeping from several wounds. My stomach churned.

"Wait, please!" Cortney cried out when we opened the trunk. "You can't just leave me in here. I can't fuckin' breathe."

"Does it look like I really give a fuck?" Leonard snarled. "Either breathe, or die. Don't make me no difference."

We tossed O-Dawg's body in the trunk and slammed the door closed. Watching Leonard work had a profound effect on me. I could see the goon he used to be. I wanted that. I wanted to be respected by young and old as the one not to be fucked with.

After wiping down Cortney's house as best we could, we went to the Cimarron River. Leonard drove down a seemingly never-ending narrow trail. Occasionally, the car bottomed out on the uneven terrain. To avoid being seen by anyone, Leonard navigated through the night using only the parking lights.

We stopped when we came to a small clearing. Beyond the thicket up ahead, the thunderous roar of rushing water pierced the night.

"We'll take turns digging until the job is done," Leonard told me. "The hole only gotta be deep enough to fit one person in it."

I was confused. "But, wh-wh-what about C-C-Cortney and her daughter?"

"If we kill them bitches, it's gon' be trouble. Big trouble."

"What's the p-p-point in burying one, if we just gon' let the others go?"

Leonard looked as if that was a stupid question to be asking. "To hide the body," he replied sarcastically. "Don't nobody give a damn about a wannabe drug dealer being killed. But if you lay a finger on that white bitch or her little girl, it's gon' feel like Armageddon done begun."

His line of reasoning didn't make sense. Just because we knew where Cortney's parents lived, worked, and done everything else-didn't mean we should take the chance of her telling.

When it was all said and done, we buried O-Dawg alive. I could still hear him whimpering as I threw dirt over his head. To make matters more traumatizing, Leonard made Cortney join in on burying O—Dawg. He wanted her to know what it felt like to bury someone she loved. If the day ever came that she felt like snitching, she'd have to bury her entire family in the same manner.

Chapter 7
Stutter

Not long after my parents quit fighting, the delicious aroma of breakfast filled the air. I moseyed on down stairs to find Momma next to the stove scrambling eggs. Her eye was puffy. Her hair looked a mess. She looked like she'd been up all night.

"M-m-morning, Momma," I said. "You w-want me to finish cooking so you can lay down and get some rest?"

She tried to smile, but the pain must've been unbearable. She winced and patted the back of my hand. That was her way of saying she could handle it.

"Whatever happened with that job interview you boys were supposed to have went to?" Leonard asked. He strolled in to the kitchen as if he didn't have a care in the world. He walked over to the refrigerator and opened it. Half a stick of butter, an empty carton of milk, and two-month-old lunch meat stared back at him. He slammed the door shut.

"I g-g-got hired," I replied.

Leonard applauded. "Good. Hope that means you fixin' to be bringing in some extra dough. Bills are overdue. We need food. The house need fixin'. Er'body gotta pitch in to make this thing work."

I turned on the faucet and got a glass of water. As bad as I wanted to remind him that I had been pitching in, I just let it go. From the looks of Momma's face, he was looking for a fight.

"W-we supposed to start working in a couple of weeks. DP gotta line th-th-things out for us."

Leonard seemed to ponder something for a moment. "How much y'all supposed to be gettin' paid?"

I shrugged. "D-d-don't know yet. S-s-sometimes the shop might be slow."

"The shop?"

I nodded.

"This nigga own a shop, but don't know how much he is going to pay his workers? Sounds to me like somebody is gettin' shafted. You gon' end up doing a whole lotta work for a little bit of money."

For me to respond would only make things more difficult. If Leonard had any idea about what I was involved in, he'd want parts. I had to be careful what I exposed to him, and even more careful about what I said. Out of all the missions I'd been on with him, I never received more than $500. While he used his to do whatever he pleased with, mine was for bills, food, and if the house needed fixin'. This was my first chance to stand on my own two feet.

"If slavin' for nickels and dimes is how you want to spend your life, that's fine by me," Leonard said. "But if I'm fixin' to be out there puttin' my life on the line while you pussyfootin' with this new gig, it's only right I get half." He paused and stared at me with a blank expression. Slowly, a familiar look formed on his face. I'd seen it the night he shot at me. I looked at Momma to make sure she saw what I had. She had.

"L!" she exclaimed and removed the skillet from the flame. "Let's go to the back room so I can talk to you."

He never broke eye contact with me. He sat glaring at me as if I were the scum of the earth. When Momma walked in his line of sight, he laughed.

"You startin' to look just like that nigga," he said.

"Leonard!" Momma snapped.

He glared up at her with contempt. "Bitch, don't you dare fix your mouth to say shit to me! This is your fault. If you'd have never fucked that nigga, this shit wouldn't be happening."

In the back of my mind, the fussing and fighting would soon be over. O-Dawg was dead. Although I had no idea why Leonard hated me so much, I would soon find out.

Chapter 8
Harold

Something about today felt different. Can't say whether it was because the weekend was just around the corner, or if my mind was playing tricks on me.

Thursday nights were meeting nights for me. I attended the Kingdom Hall from 7-9 and listened to the brothers share the Good News. Lotta folks don't believe the Good News is the truth, but I do, 'cause that's exactly what it is. The Truth.

As usual, I invited Kevin to tag along. He wouldn't. I imagine the loss of his best friend hit him harder than anything he ever felt. All he do is mope around the house, doing nothing. Every once and awhile, he'll disappear in the streets for an hour or two, then come back home looking like a lost puppy. I tried to help him understand that death is just a part of life. You can't have one without the other. At least, not in this system of things. Course, Kevin didn't have time to be hearing talk like that. He was too busy chasing the dream of how to be a fool. I had to be careful how I dealt with him. Too much talk about The Truth was like shining a light on a roach. The last thing I wanted to do was push him further away from me. The best thing I could think to do was let go and let God.

At 6:45. I was out the door. Meeting nights were something special, not only because of the Good News I heard, but because I was also one step closer to the weekend. The weekend was my time to catch up on a little relaxation, a little tinkering with my cars, watch TV, mow the lawn. A little of everything. Saturdays, I went out in field service. Part of knowing the truth meant I had to spread it.

Flickering headlights in my rearview caught my attention. Why someone would be flagging me down on a day like today, was beyond my understanding. Everyone that knew me knew that tonight was a meeting night. Whoever was flagging me down must didn't know. I pulled in the F&H parking lot and waited.

F&H was a family owned mini-market that had been there since I was a kid. The parking lot was only big enough for 10 to 12 cars, all parked alongside each other. Today, the parking lot was empty. Business hours were from 7 a.m.-5 p.m. Monday-Friday. Had the store owner, Mr. Franklin, been around, he'd have insisted I moved.

A burgundy Lincoln pulled in on my passenger side. I strained, trying to get a good look inside. The windows were tinted. Not many people drove that model car in that condition. One of the front tires was a small spare tire, and the car was covered in dirt. I vaguely recall seeing that car somewhere, just couldn't remember exactly where. When the driver's door opened, I instantly knew who it was.

"Wait!" Leonard barked.

I slammed my truck in reverse and tried to back out of the parking lot. Had I not been so worried about hitting him, I'd have kept going. "Get away from my truck?" I shouted.

Leonard glared at me and then marched behind my truck and just stood there.

"I ain't in the mood to be playin', Leonard. I'll run yo' behind over and leave you dead in the street." I revved up the engine to let I know I meant business.

He didn't budge.

"What is it?" I hopped out and stormed to the back of my truck to face him like a man. Just the sight of him made me sick. I hated him. He wore the same dirty blue jeans he'd been in for the last twenty years and his shoes looked like the same one's his daddy bought him when he was fourteen.

"Calm down," Leonard said smoothly. "I didn't stop you because I wanted to argue. I stopped you, because I wanna share the Good News with you."

"You goin' ta' hell for that. The only Good News you could tell me was that you moving to Africa to fight lions."

"Wishful thinking. Seriously, though. I finally figured out who those new fellas in town are. They're some old friends of yours. You've known them since back in the day."

"Hear me, and hear me clearly. The only friends I've got are Jehovah's Witnesses. I don't mess with no dope selling, crack smoking thugs that are on their way to prison. Unless you want to be the first one out y'all's little group to end up in a jail cell— I suggest you find someone else to share your Good News with."

Leonard laughed. "You make that shit sound *sooo* believable. Like you're this upstanding citizen that ain't neva done no wrong. You might got everyone else fooled, but I know betta."

"You don't know jack squat 'bout me!"

"I know we committed every sin you can think of and ain't no way you can make that right with God. Nigga, we flipped bricks together." He inched closer and swiped at his nose. "We counted millions together." He inched closer, his lips just inches from my ear. "We buried bodies together. How the fuck you gon' fix your mouth to say I don't know you?"

This was exactly why nobody liked a crackhead. Whenever they ran out of dope, that's when the dirt comes out. All that mess he was talking happened back in the day. I been put that stuff behind me. It's in God's hands now. "You said all of that to say what, Leonard? Do you want $20?" I whipped out my wallet and fished out a crisp twenty-dollar bill. "Here."

"I don't want your gotdamn money!"

"Then what do you want? The stuff you talkin' 'bout happened a *looong* time ago. It's done. Over. I got baptized." I threw my hands in the air. "I'm saved."

"You going to hell right along with the rest of us," Leonard snarled. "You might got everybody else fooled, but I can see through your smoke screen. You's still the same low-down snake you've always been."

"Well, if that's what you see, back off!"

He chuckled. "There goes the muthafucka that I know." He pulled out a gun and let it hang down by his side." And what's gon' happen if I don't back off?" I started to walk off, but then I recognized the gun that he had. It was mine. "What in God's name are you still doing with that thing? You were supposed to get rid of that thang a long time ago."

"I did get rid of it," he said. "It just kept coming back. I figured God was trying to tell me something, so I held on to it. Never know, might come in handy one day."

Leonard must've got a hold of some seriously powerful stuff this time. Nobody in their right mind would say or do the things he does. "Leonard, now I don't know what kinda drugs you done got a hold of, and frankly, I don't care. From this day forward, I want you to stay the hell away from me. I'm going down to the station, first thing in the morning, to file a restraining order on you."

"Be my guest! Make sure and tell 'em I held you at gunpoint with your gun." He looked around as if he'd accidentally revealed some deep dark secret. My bad. Wasn't supposed to say that, was I? If the wrong people found out about this, I'm sure there'd be hell to pay. Folks gon' know how crooked you've always been."

Enough was enough. My tolerance for his foolishness had reached its limit. I'd said all I needed to say. I went back to get in my truck. Just as soon as I opened the door, he said, "I plan on stopping by to see your old friend, Cabbage."

"Praise God! Hop in. I'll give you a lift."

He laughed. "You never cease to amaze me. One minute you want me to stay away from you. The next, you wanna give me a lift to the crack house."

"If you want to be stupid enough to go 'round there messing with them people, have at it. All I can do is send you with the Lord's Prayer. Yea, though I walk——"

"You keep thinking it's a game. Just because you're my brother don't mean I won't put that ass on ice."

"Go on and do whatever you feel you need to do. I'm tired of your threats and I'm tired of looking at your face." I got back in the truck and slammed the door. This time when I hit reverse, he moved. He must've seen it in my eyes. We were done. Whatever happened next was in God's hands.

Chapter 9
Kevin

The first night after we had robbed Bill, my mind started playing tricks on me. Every sound that I heard I thought was the laws coming to get me.

My father didn't want me getting tangled up in O-Dawg's beef. He kept a close eye on me. "What are you doing?" he asked.

I had got up to look out the living room window. "Did you just see—" I moved a little to the left, a little more to the right. "Never mind. I must've been tripping."

When day 2 rolled around, I was seeing stuff, but couldn't tell you what. I was hearing things, but couldn't quite tell you what I heard.

"Kevin!" my father snapped. "You can't keep jumping up and running to the window every five minutes. You gon' have to get a grip. What's wrong with you?"

I peered out into the darkness, beyond where our porch light could reach. Someone was out there. I just knew it. "Did you see how the lights just flickered?"

My father looked at the lamp, at the dining room light, at the television. "Nope. Must've missed it."

"It happened right when I saw a shadow shoot across the porch."

My father got up to have a look for himself. He peered through the blinds into the night. He moved a little to the left, a little more to the right. "Don't see nothing," he said. "You sure you saw something?"

I know what I saw and I know what I heard. With each passing day, paranoia had a tighter hold on me. By the end of the first week, I was ready to tell my father everything. What happened. Who did what. Where, when, and then. I was scared to death. I kept waking up in the middle of the night in cold sweats.

My father came in my bedroom when he noticed my light was on. "Boy, what are you doing up this time of night?" he snapped.

I started pacing. "I'm scared."

He looked alarmed. "Of who?"

I wasn't so sure I wanted to tell him everything. Being scared was good enough.

"Kevin, do you hear me talking to you?"

I sighed. "Sorry. I'm just hungry."

"You hungry? We just ate a couple of hours ago. If you hungry, go in there and fix you some noodles or something. It's some lunch meat in there. Fix you a sandwich."

"I heard they eat noodles in jail."

"Do it matter what they eat in jail?" I shook my head. "Well don't be asking what they eat in jail. Sounds like you're tuned in on the wrong frequency. Change the channel. You might have a better outcome."

Any other time, I'd shut him down quick when he got to talking in parables and metaphors. But that night, I needed that shit. Maybe his words of wisdom might keep me from spending the rest of my life in prison.

Homicide scoured through every nook and cranny Guthrie had to offer. With O-Dawg's murder added to the list of growing unsolved mysteries, people in high places wanted answers. Cops put the squeeze on the streets and left no stone unturned. Every dope house from the east side to the west side shut down shop. Cabbage and his crew had long since skipped town. Reality finally settled in. We were exposed.

"I've been thinking," I began by saying. "It can't be a good idea for us to be sitting out here in the open if everyone else is laying low. Out of sight, out of mind. Ain't that what Leonard used to say to us?"

A sheriff's truck turned the corner next to Stutters house. The truck slowed as the driver eyed us with suspicion. No matter how many times that had happened, I couldn't help but think they knew what we had done.

"Fuck them!" Stutter growled. "They can ride back and forth all they want. T-t-that just proves w-w-we're here. Like we've always been."

As much as I wanted to agree with him, I couldn't. There were four of us that went to rob Bill. No telling who saw what, who slipped up and done what, or who left what behind that would connect us all to the scene of the crime.

"I wish I could look at things the way you do. Maybe it'd be easier for me to forget that night."

We silently watched as the sheriff's truck topped the hill. Any day, any second, that could be us being hauled away in the back.

"Do you think you'll ever forget what you done?"

Stutter looked at me as if he had to be reminded of what I was talking about.

"You shot three people—"

The front door opened behind us. Leonard stepped out on the porch. He lifted his collar, cuffed his lighter, and lit a cigarette. "Gettin' too cold to be sittin' out here in the cold like this," he said. "Be a shame if one of y'all get sick before things finally get back to normal."

Stutter nudged me in the side, signaling for me to keep cool. If Leonard was worried about anything we were doing, he was probably fishing for information.

"We just out here watching to see what the rollers are up to," I explained. "Every five minutes, they hit the corner. I suppose whatever happened out on Waterloo Road got the streets lit."

Leonard hit his cigarette and let the smoke seep from his nose. "Don't matter what the cops got going on," he said." Y'all gotta find a way to keep looking normal. Don't be fooled into thinking don't nobody know what happened or don't nobody know what's going on. That's the furthest thing from the truth. Always stay sharp and don't tell nobody what you've done." He strolled down the steps with not so much as another word.

The miserable state of paranoia I'd been in came back with vengeance. Did he know something? Did someone tell him something?

"We've gotta get outta here," I said to Stutter.

He smirked. "W-w-what for?"

"You didn't hear what that nigga just said? Your old man don't just be saying anything. If he said something, that must mean he knows something. I say we go lay low for a while to give the heat a chance to die down."

"T-t-that's easy for you to say. Y-y-you can go hide out in Florida with your mom. I gotta stay here and deal with whatever happens."

"If you ain't down to go nowhere, then I ain't leaving, either. Besides, I don't have the money to leave town. Hopefully I will after we holla at DP."

Stutter appeared intrigued. "Y-you talked to him, yet?"

"Last night."

Stutter scoffed. "W-why you didn't say anything?"

I shrugged. "I don't know. Maybe, because we don't see things the same. While you over here worried about some money, I'm stressing on whether or not we gon' get caught!" Everything I just said seemed to go right over his head.

"D-d-did he say anything about our money? It's been three whole weeks. He should h-have our m-m-money by now."

"He didn't say nothing about any money. All he kept talking 'bout was be at the shop tonight. He supposed to have a surprise for us."

"What kind of-of-of surprise?"

I couldn't do nothing but shake my head. Stutter must've been starving. I thought being broke was hard. I could never imagine what it felt like to be him. All I know is to be at the shop by 9. Everythang else, we about to find out when we get there.

***

Later that night...

I parked in front of DP's shop just like before. The only difference between then and now, there were no lights on inside the building.

"Don't it feel funny to be out here this time of night?" I asked.

Stutter scanned the inside of the shop as well. His usual calm was more alert. "It do f-f-feel kinda strange," he stammered. "It almost m-m-make me-me feel like we're b-b-being watched."

The gentle clatter of a fence drew our attention towards it. The gate on the side of the building had opened. Moments later, Sip stepped into view. "Pull your car in the shop!" he instructed me. As we drove past him, I couldn't help but notice how hard he was shining. He wore a thick gold chain with diamond loop earrings.

"Where's the homie?" I asked as we got out.

Sip hit a button and closed the garage door. "He should be here any second," he said. " He wanted you to park inside because we all rollin' with him tonight."

That idea must didn't sit right with Stutter. He stopped in the middle of my path, causing me to bump into him. "Where w-w-we supposed to be going?" Stutter asked.

"Beats me," Sip replied. "The only time I ask questions is when there's money involved." Sip left us in the lounge area while he went to handle something up front.

As soon as the office door closed, Stutter was in my ear. "D-d-did. you see-see that big-ass diamond ring?" he asked. "He wasn't wearing none of that stuff th-the last time we were here."

I smiled and shook my head. If it wasn't something about money, then it was about someone trying to get over on some money. "I know what you're gettin' at," I told him. "These niggas ain't got no reason to try and play us. They're the ones that made it to where we could come up. They been getting money."

The garage door began to open and the headlights of a white SUV came into view. We couldn't see more than the front fender and rim. Since we knew DP was on the way, we went to have a look. An all-white Escalade limousine stretched beyond the fence. The driver opened the back door and DP slid out.

"What the business is?" he exclaimed. "You niggas ready to go set the city on fire, or what?"

I was stuck on stupid. I hadn't ever seen no shit like that in my life. As far as I knew, limousines were for funerals, rappers, and movie stars.

"Look at us! We ain't dressed to do nothing. Stutter look like he been grindin' on the block for three days and I know I'm not too far behind him."

DP held up two small wads of money and said, "Fuck them clothes. Here's $2500 apiece. That's two thousand for the job and another 500 for your troubles. So is you niggas comin' or what?"

He didn't have to ask us twice. We were out!

While I was excited as shit to be riding in a limousine, I couldn't really say for Stutter. For the most part, he rode in silence with his hood on. I guess with three bodies weighing in on my conscience, I'd be doing the same thing. Not to mention he'd been beyond broke for I don't know how long. Hopefully, the money he just got paid would help him.

The first place we stopped at was at a restaurant called Trappers. Trappers was a branch of Red Lobster, specializing in seafood and fine dining. We ordered crab legs, lobster tails, steak...the works! Stutter didn't even know how to eat half the shit. He had to watch how one of us peeled the shell of a shrimp before he could devour them. I thought Sip and DP would try and clown the homie, but instead, they embraced him. They taught him how to pop bottles like a boss and drink champagne straight from the bottle.

After we finished eating, we hit club Lexus. The same effect the limousine had on me was the same one it had on everyone else. The parking lot was a Walmart-sized parking lot, with bumper-to-bumper traffic. Devin The Dude was having a concert at the club that night. His tour bus was parked VIP in front of the club. DP instructed the driver to pull up behind them.

"I don't know if security will let me park behind those cones," the driver said. "But I'll sure as hell give it a try."

By the time we'd looped around to where the tour bus was, people thought that we were with Devin The Dude. The limousine we were in was new to the city. No one had rented it and only a handful had seen it. Luckily, the owner was a close business associate of DP's. He let him use the limousine any time.

Security allowed us to park behind the tour bus with no problem. When our driver opened the door, a security guard said, "Y'all stick together. We gon' try to get you in and up front as quick as possible."

They led us inside the club and we began our journey to the stage. Girls tugged at our clothes, hands, practically anything they could get their hands on. I wanted to holla at every last one of them, but I didn't want to be exposed, either. We weren't who they thought we were. They obviously thought we were famous.

"It can be like this every day if you want it to be," DP told me. "When you handle your business, ain't nothing you can't have. Ain't a bitch you can't knock. Ain't a car you can't have. Yeah, it's gonna be a bunch of niggas that start hatin' but tell me, is it worth it?"

As I looked around, if I wasn't catching a smirk or a mean mug, then some chick was all up in my grill. With all the new attention, I couldn't help but think about LaShura. What would she think of me if she could see me now? I hadn't seen her in a few weeks. The way I felt that night, I wanted the world to see me.

"Would it be cool if we stopped by to see O-Dawg's sister?" I asked DP. "I want her to see me in that big pretty muthafucka before you gotta turn it back in."

DP laughed at me and said, "You still don't get it, do you? This is what we do! Every day gon' feel like Christmas once you get your money right. You need to really ask yourself, is this something that I want to do? 'Cause all this shit right here—" he panned his hand over the room, "—come with the job. Just stick with me. I'll show you how shit really go."

I was listening, but then I wasn't. To keep it all the way one hunnit, this lifestyle wasn't the route I was trying to go. Stutter had just killed three people. We were lucky to have gotten away with it. Ain't no way I would keep pushing my luck. The only thing I needed to figure out was how long I'd lay low at Pops'.

At 2 a.m., the lights inside the club came on. "I don't know where y'all going," the DJ yelled over the microphone, " but y'all got to get the hell outta here!"

Boos erupted from the crowd. Some tossed trash at the stage while everyone else made their way to the door.

Security ushered us back out to the limousine with no problem. Everyone that was inside the club now gathered around the orange cones that were spaced around us. When the driver saw us, he opened the door for us to get in.

Cameras clicked away. Even people on the tour bus had stepped off to see who we were.

Just as we started to climb inside the limousine, a woman shouldered her way through the crowd and said," Can I please take a picture with you?"

It took a moment

for it to register that she was talking to me. Course, everyone gladly posed for the camera. Even Stutter was with it.

As more and more people began to press in on us, Security advised us to leave.

Chapter 10
LaShura

The decision to move in with Nikki turned out to be the best thing I could've done. The change of scenery and pace worked wonders for me psychologically, whereas before, I felt drained and didn't want to do anything. Now, it was hard for me to sit still. I had energy only if it pertained to doing me. Getting my life in order so I could finally have peace of mind. My mother's house may have seemed peaceful, on the outside looking in - if you considered your uncle sneaking around at night, going through your purse in search of money, peaceful, then maybe it was time to redefine what peace meant.

The illusion of peace I so masterfully created was exposed the moment I changed my surroundings. The negative things I had internalized as normal could no longer distract me. I could feed on positive energy and focus on me.

Vance and Nikki lived in a two-bedroom. apartment on the northside of Oklahoma City. They'd been saving up to buy a house since we graduated college. Vance was an accountant for a small car dealership. Nikki worked in home health care. I didn't want a job in my profession until I felt more in control of my feelings. What good could I be for someone else if I was no good for me?

The other day, Vance offered me a job at the dealership.

"Doing what?" I'd asked. We'd been brainstorming on what I wanted to do since the first night I moved in. Nikki's suggestion was home healthcare.

Vance seemed reluctant to say. "Customer service," he finally said. "I know for certain I could get you on there. People generally take those type of jobs until something better comes along. But it's a start."

The first thing I had to ask myself was, do I want to deal with people all day? Do I want to talk to people all day? Do I need some money? "I'll do it."

Vance appeared excited. "For real?" he said. "Just stop by and put in an application. I'll start the process on my end and we'll go from there."

With a job secured and a temporary roof over my head, now all I needed was my own car. Momma had offered to cosign one for me, but I couldn't. How could I? The struggle was real for us both. If she needed me, I'd do whatever I could. But for now, I was determined to stand on my own two feet. If I couldn't get what I needed by using my own resources, then I didn't need it.

Kevin called to check on me several times a day. Every morning when he woke up, it was the same scenario.

My phone rang.

"Hello." Silence. Heavy breathing. "Hello!"

"Oh, umm. What'chu doing?" Kevin asked in a groggy voice, as if I'd just woke him up.

"I'm asleep. What do you think I'm doing? It's 6:30 in the morning. What's wrong?"

He blew his nose. "I got up to get a glass of water." He fell silent.

"And?"

"I thought about you."

"You thought about what, Kevin?"

He fell silent for a moment. "Us," he finally replied.

"Stop playing before I hang up this phone."

"Girl, ain't nobody playin' wit'chu. Don't start acting like that."

"Start acting like what?"

"Like that! One minute we was cool. Chilling. We smoked weed together."

"You offered a few times and I said yeah. And?"

"What about when I spent the night?"

"You told my mother you wanted to stick around and help out. I never asked you to spend the night.

"What about when we held hands?"

"Held hands? When?"

"When we prayed."

Click.

Stupid, stupid, stupid. You can't just say it once if it pertains to Kevin. You have to say it three times. Abnormal conversations is what I got when I talked to him. We might reminisce about James, then the conversation would take an abrupt turn to the left.

My phone rang.

"What!" I snapped.

"Calm down," he spoke smoothly. "It's me, Kevin."

"You don't think I know who's calling? It seems like you're the only one that calls. You call every day at the same times to ask the same stupid questions."

"Oh, so the questions I be asking you, be stupid?"

I sighed heavily. "What did I just say, Kevin?"

He chuckled while mumbling something under his breath. I heard a bag rustle, then open. I assumed that he'd opened a bag of chips, by the sound of the crunching he was doing. "You ate yet?" he asked.

"No. Why?"

"'Cause I'm fixin' to slide through and bring you something to eat."

"I don't need you to slide through and bring me nothing. Nikki don't want you hanging around her house."

"Nikki ain't talkin' 'bout nothin'. Don't nobody wanna be hanging around her house no way. What we gon' chill and do? Talk about the bible?"

"Is this what you called to do?"

"What?"

"Get on my nerves."

"So I'm gettin' on your nerves now?"

"What do you want, Kevin?"

He must've grabbed a handful of chips and chomped down on them. All I could hear was him smacking, then he must've washed it down with something. "Ahhhh" he hissed. "Do you love me."

Click.

I slammed the phone down in his face. I hope I busted his eardrum. Stupid. Stupid, stupid, stupid. Whatever was going on in Guthrie had everyone acting strange.

Outside of Kevin's abnormal conversations, Uncle Tim hadn't been home in days. Momma thought it had something to do with the police. She said they been riding past the house every fifteen minutes.

I clicked off the television and got up. I'd been laying around watching TV all morning. I had to get out. Do something. Go somewhere. See something!

The Chevy Beretta Nikki drove back in college was what I used whenever she didn't need it. That day, I decided to go to the grocery store. We didn't need much, just a few items. I figured this would be the perfect opportunity to simply browse the aisles.

"I miss you," a familiar voice said.

I hadn't been in the store five minutes and Stanley was already on my heels.

"You should've thought about what could happen before you cheated on me." I tried to open the refrigerator door and get a gallon of milk, but he blocked my path. "Stanley, move."

He held up his hands in surrender. "I don't want to argue," he said. "And I damn sure didn't come here to fight."

"Then can you please move so I can get what I came in here to get?"

"Only if we can talk?"

I sighed and rolled my eyes. "About what, Stanley? Toyia? Is that what you stopped me to talk about?"

"I stopped you to let you know, I'm not ready to give this up. I made a tiny mistake."

"A tiny mistake? You call sleeping with some other woman a tiny mistake?" I shoved him aside and grabbed a gallon of milk. My mind kept telling me to get the cheese, stop and get some bread, and go! My body must've been set on doing its own thing. I marched straight down the aisle and started grabbing stuff. Cheese, ice cream, yogurt.

"Since when did you start eating yogurt?" Stanley inquired.

"Since when did you care what I ate? All you need to be worried about is what you and Toyia eat." I didn't even like yogurt. I grabbed it because he was carrying everything. I was there to grab only a few items. When he showed up…chicken, hot dogs, steak.

"LaShura, stop!" Stanley snapped. "You don't even have a basket. That's how I know you didn't come here to buy all of this stuff."

"Just cause I don't have a basket doesn't mean I didn't come here to buy all of this. Maybe I just forgot the basket." I headed to the checkout. I added a bag of chips and a few packs of Starburst to the pile.

When we arrived at the checkout, I couldn't help but notice the look on the cashier's face. I added a couple of magazines to see if that might prompt her to say something.

"Babe, whatever I gotta do to get you to come home, I'll do it," Stanley said. "I'm tired of being at home without you. I need you back in my life."

"I don't think I'm ready for that just yet. I need some time alone. Maybe go out and be with someone else like you did."

"Now you're being unrealistic. You know I won't allow none of that. The only reason I allowed things to go this far was on the strength of what happened to your brother."

"You keep saying allowed. Boy, please. What makes you think you can allow me to do anything?"

He sighed heavily.

The cashier cleared her throat. "That'll be $72.60. Would you like to pay in cash, or credit card?"

I had to replay everything over from the beginning. When we first walked up, she kept giving us these funny looks. When she told me the total, it almost seemed like she had an attitude. I glanced down at her name tag. Toyia.

"So this is who you've been sleeping with?"

Stanley's jaw dropped. "Babe, you trippin'."

"No, I'm not tripping. Is this who you've been sleeping with?"

"I don't even know him!" the cashier chimed in.

"Well, you've been all up in his face like you know him. You been all up in my face, for that matter."

"Look, are y'all going to pay for these groceries or not? Either pay for the items and leave, or step aside while I get my manager to help you."

Stanley tried to rub my back, thinking it would calm me down. I shoved him off me.

"Don't touch me!"

He whipped out his wallet and paid for the groceries. The cashier didn't say thank you, or nothing when she gave Stanley his change. She eyed me with a funky look as we walked out the store.

"The only reason I'm here was to see you." Stanley said. "I was on my way to Nikki's when I saw you leave in her car."

"Why were you on your way to Nikki's?"

"To see you."

"Are you crazy?"

"Whatever I gotta do to keep from losing you, I'm going to do it. That shit with Toyia is done. We don't ever have to even bring her up again. I proved to you that I didn't have nothing to do with what happened to your brother."

"No. You could've paid someone to do it." I popped the trunk for him to put the bags inside. He simply stood there.

"Stop sayin' dumb shit like that," he spat.

"I'm just telling you the way I feel. If you don't wanna hear what I feel, then don't talk to me."

He laughed forcefully and put the bags in the trunk. "I'm going to take that," he said. "This time. I deserve some of your frustration, but not all of it. Sooner or later you're gonna have to move on from this. I'm not going nowhere. The longer you hold onto that shit with Toyia, the longer it'll continue to hold us back."

I guess that was supposed to be his grand closing statement. He walked away with not so much as another word. Honestly, what more was there to say? He said what he said. I believed what I wanted to and that was the end of it.

All that stuff about Toyia went in one ear and out the other. I didn't believe the reason he was there, either. Stanley would never think it was okay to show up at Nikki's apartment. Impossible. He shot her. The crazy thing is, out of all the things that he said that I didn't believe, I believed him at "I miss you".

I was gone. Torn between love and hate. I wanted to believe that he loved me. I wanted to know this was a mistake and would never happen again. I wanted to take him back so badly. I needed him. I wanted him.

I hurried back to Nikki's from the grocery store, my thoughts racing all over the place. When I walked in Nikki's apartment, she instantly knew something was wrong.

"Girl, what happened?" Nikki said.

"Nothing," I replied. I set a couple of bags down on the table while Vance went to get the others.

"I know you. Something's up. You've got that look on your face."

Stanley, Stanley, Stanley. I couldn't stop thinking about Stanley. Of course, I couldn't talk to my best friend about that, because she'd probably think I was insane. I told her that my stomach had been cramping so I'd spend the rest of the day in bed. The later it got, I started looking forward to Kevin calling. He called every day around the same time. His abnormal conversations and remarks were a part of my normal. He'd been that way since I'd known him. When 11 o'clock rolled around, I guessed he wouldn't call. I dozed off, only to be woken up at 3 o'clock in the morning. The house phone was ringing off the hook.

"Come outside," a caller slurred when I answered the phone.

"Do what?"

"Come outside!" he stated forcefully.

"Who is this?"

"This yo' muthafuckin' boyfriend. Now come outside!"

I sniffled. My nose was itching. I sat up. Double checked the clock. This fool was definitely tripping. Only one person in the whole wide world would be dumb enough to call someone at this time of morning. Stupid.

"Kevin, you can't be calling here at this time of night," I said to him. "People have jobs around here. They also like to sleep too."

"Come outside!"

Click. He hung up in my face.

While I was sitting there trying to wrap my mind around what had just happened, there was a knock at the door. Nikki peeked inside my room.

"Did you see that big limousine parked out front? It's blocking traffic."

Then it hit me. Stupid, stupid, stupid. Come outside! I jumped up and ran to the window. Sure enough, it was him.

"I'm sorry. I'll handle it."

Nikki gasped. "You know who that is?"

I nodded. "It's Kevin. I don't know why he's here. Don't care. I didn't tell him he could stop by, either. Don't worry. I'll take care of it." I slipped on my house coat and headed for the door. Nikki was hot on my heels. She knew how Kevin was. Everyone know how Kevin was. Vance went back to bed, refusing to entertain his shenanigans.

When we went downstairs, Kevin was already standing outside waiting for us." What in the world has gotten in to you?" Nikki snarled.

"You," he replied.

"You've been beggin' for it for a long time. Haven't you little boy?" She tugged at the straps on her headwrap and started swinging her arms back and forth. Kevin brought something out of her. He brought something out of us all.

I stepped in between them. "Nikki, I'll handle this."

She swung. He swatted it down effortlessly.

"Why are you out here drunk at this time in the morning?"

Kevin sipped champagne straight from the bottle and staggered towards us. I stopped him by placing my hand on his chest.

"'Cause, I wanted you to see this limo. Ain't this shit dope?"

"That doesn't make it alright just to pop up at all times of the night, Kevin. Besides, whose limousine is this?"

He smirked and took a swig. "It's mine!"

Stupid, stupid, stupid. "Why do you always gotta lie? Can you please just tell me that?"

A couple of cars honked as they drove around. Kevin waved back, as if their verbal assaults and middle fingers were gestures of kindness.

"We got plenty of weed and drank if you tryin' to roll," Kevin said.

Nikki slid back in between us. "If *who's* trying to roll?" she spat. "The only one that's gon' be rolling anywhere tonight is you!"

While they started back bickering, I went to have a look inside the limousine. The back door was open, plus I'd never been inside one. Just as I neared the rear of the limo, I saw Stanley's car pass by. I know he had to see me too. Everyone saw me.

"That nigga betta keep right on doin' what he was doin'," Kevin snarled as he approached. "He must ain't got his goons with him to back him up. That should show you what type of hoe-ass nigga he is."

I was listening to Kevin, but then again, I wasn't. I needed answers. Why was he there? Would he disrespect my best friend, knowing damn well she didn't like him?

***

Kevin

The day after our night out at the club, I was back in the city to see LaShura. Besides her not having closure on who killed her brother, Stanley was spotted leaving Nikki's apartments. While I chalked it up as his way of checking in on LaShura, she suspected it was something more.

"It's not a coincidence that he was here last night," LaShura said. "He was over here doing something. I just can't figure out what it was."

I sparked up a blunt and inhaled deeply. "Maybe he wanted to see who was in the limo." LaShura rolled her eyes at me as I exhaled the smoke. "I'm serious! You should've seen all those people taking pictures of us. They thought we were superstars."

"Do you really think Stanley would follow y'all all the way over here, just to see who is in that limo?"

"Hell yeah. You already know how the nigga be hatin'."

She snickered. "So, Stanley be hatin' on you?"

"Duuuh. You know he do. If it wasn't for all that sneak dissin' he be doin', me and you would've been together."

"Boy, please. It won't neva be no me and you."

I looked at her like she was crazy. "Yeah, it will."

"No, it won't."

"Why not?"

"Because I'm too old for you."

"Girl, please."

"Whateva."

"Whatever then."

"You stupid."

"You is too."

I tried to pass her the blunt, but she wouldn't take it.

"I can't get high anymore," she said. "Vance got me a job working at the car lot where he works."

Chapter 11
Harold

The situation between me and my brother had to change. Something had to give. I couldn't continue to hold on to the past just because he didn't want to let it go. Leonard dangled my dirty secrets over my head as if they were his golden ticket to God only knows where. I left all my burdens in God's hands and never looked back. What we did happened decades ago, it was probably eating at his conscience.

Dealing with my brother was like dealing with a wild animal. You never knew what to expect. It wasn't so much that I was worried about what he'd do to me. My main concern was for Kevin. I couldn't allow him to get blindsided by foolishness, because he ain't got sense enough to know when something is coming. My best friend says we all like walking magnets. We attract good and bad situations and things to us. He says if we pay real close attention to what's goin' on around you, you could get a better read on what's headed your direction. When I think about what he'd said and take into consideration the way I've been feeling, something bad was about to happen. Since Kevin wasn't at home, this would be a fine time to sort through this mess and figure out what I'm gon' do.

I flipped through several channels, hoping to find something to watch. Nothing was on but daytime soaps, the news, and a few game shows. I used part of my vacation time to take a few days off. I planned on spending a little time with Kevin to see where his head was at. By the time I woke up that morning, he was gone. I knew he'd been chasing after that O'Dell girl here lately. I figured he must've got an early start on her trail. When you find the one you like, you can't let 'em get away.

I moseyed on into the kitchen and opened the cabinets. A bottle of Jack Daniels stared back at me. Rarely did I ever touch the stuff, only on special occasions. Alcohol, at one time or another, had me in a bad way. It took some hard work to shake free of the hold it had on me. Nowadays, I only drink once in a blue moon. Can't ever let myself drift back to where I was. I had to keep my mind sharp. Focused.

I poured another double shot and knocked it back. Poured another and knocked it back too. I wondered what Kevin was doing. Where was he? Was he safe? Would he be home later that evening? I went back to my recliner and settled in. Course I brought my shot glass and bottle of JD. Since nothing was on television, I figured I'd listen to some jazz to set this thing off right. Nowadays, it don't take much to get me where I'm going. I can drink a little bit, and before I knew it, I'd be passed out asleep. Back when I was growing up, I could drink a whole pint of liquor by myself.

I smiled. Knocked another one back. Maybe that's why I have lasted so long. The fact that it never took me much to get where I was going. Grandpa told me to keep that mentality in everything I do. Touch and move. Touch and move. As soon as you get stuck, unable to let go, that's when the bad starts happening. That very reason was why I wanted to be like Kenny when I was growing up.

Kenny was the oldest, but not the brightest. In Momma's book, he was a saint. He got good grades, graduated high school, got a good job. Thinking back to what Grandpa told me to do, Kenny was the closest thing to being a man that I knew. Outside of Grandpa, Kenny was the only man that I could relate to.

Before I moved out of Momma's house she asked, "What are you going to do with yourself?"

I shrugged. "I'on't know."

"Then, how you going to take care of yourself? You don't even know how you're going to support yourself."

"I do know how I'm going to support myself."

"Then, how?"

"Like Kenny."

Momma shook her head. "What might work for Kenny, might not work for you. You gotta figure out who you wanna be. What Harold wants to do."

All that mess she was talkin' was going in one ear and straight out the other. I was stuffing my bags full of clothes just as fast as I could. Kenny couldn't get there fast enough. This was the longest me and Momma had a sensible conversation in weeks. Now" that she finally realized. that I was leaving for good, she had to accept that the extra income would be gone as well.

"I want you to know," Momma said. "I done the best I could to raise y'all boys." I'm sure you feel otherwise, but the fact remains the same. I did my best."

And I done my best not to bust out laughing in her face. At least three times a week, we had to scrape a meal together with scraps from the neighbor's house. Momma would be out chasing after one of her many lovers. Although some of those men were the reason our lights stayed on, most of them simply used Momma for whatever they could get.

Not long after I finished packing, I waited on the porch for Kenny to arrive. Momma and Baby Leonard sat in a porch swing across from me. Baby Leonard's beady eyes roamed up and down the road. I'm sure he hated the fact that I was leaving more than Momma did. She might have spoiled him whenever she was around, but that was whenever she was around. We had to figure things out on our own.

At the top of the hill, a long white car came to a stop at the sign. I squinted, trying to get a better look. Kenny said something about a white car before, but this wasn't just any white car. This was what the gangsters drove. To see Kenny whip in the driveway ridin' in something pretty, I lost my mind. My big brother Kenny had made it big time.

"You did it!" I shouted and then jumped around. "Hot shit, mutha—"

"Don't forget where you at!" Momma warned.

Shit! Ta hell with where I was at, we'd be leaving there any moment.

Kenny had got himself a 1976 Buick Electra. It was white with two burgundy pinstripes down the side. The interior was plush burgundy material. The 30-inch white walls gave it that gangster look.

"I hope you find whateva it is you lookin' fa'," Momma said. "You been itchin' to get out on your own. Now your time has come."

In my book, we'd had our time to talk. The show was over. It was time to move on.

I loaded my things in the trunk while Kenny talked to Momma and Baby Leonard. Before we said our goodbyes, I saw Kenny give Momma a wad of money.

On the ride to Oklahoma City, I asked him about it. "I saw that wad of money you gave Momma," I told him. "You gotta be raking in some serious dough to be shellin' out duckets like that. What you done got yourself off in to? You hustlin' tables now? Sellin'? What?"

Kenny chuckled and said, "I work. Every now and then I make an extra dollar or two on the side. For the most part, I punch that clock."

"Momma says you might can get me on at Goodyear."

He nodded. "Been waiting to see if that's the direction that you want to take. It's hard work."

"Will I be able to shell out the kinda duckets you gave Momma?"

He laughed. "You gon' be able to do all that and more. But first things first. We gotta get you hired at the job. Second, once your checks start coming in, you gotta pitch in on the rent. Last but not least, you've got to get your own set of wheels. Nobody drives the white horse but me."

Kenny lived in a two-bedroom house on the south side of the city. Most of the people that lived in the area were Mexican. Kenny had rented the house because of the location and the rent was cheap. Now that I was moving in, he could save that much more money and buy more of the things he wanted.

A couple of weeks after I moved in, rumors started circulating that the warehouse was shutting down. Course I'd already put in my application and was waiting on a response. Come to find out, Kenny had his hands in several lucrative avenues to make money. Soon, his side hustles became my main hustle. I sold Black Mollies, T's and Blues, whatever I could get my hands on. Kenny wasn't too keen on the idea of me selling dope as my main source of income. But with Goodyear not responding to any of my calls and Ru's Soul

Taco's hadn't either, what else was I to do? I was doing what I had to do. Wasn't no turning back for me this time.

Most of Kenny's friends that came by the house were either white or Mexican. They'd stop by and hangout, mostly during the weekends. It wasn't uncommon for a small gathering to turn into a full-blown party. Course, that's where my expertise came in handy. I supplied all the party favorites, which enabled me to help out with the utilities. It wasn't long before our weekend parties started to spill over in to Kenny's work week. One missed day gradually became 2, and 2 quickly turned into 3. Before we knew it, Kenny had found himself in a tight spot.

"They fired you, didn't they?" I asked.

Kenny glanced over at me, then returned his gaze to the movie screen. We were at the Beacon Drive-In movie theater when I noticed his gloomy attitude had worsened.

"Just like that," Kenny began by saying. "It's over. I'm out." He forcefully chuckled.

"So, what are you gonna do now? You know we got rent and bills comin' up that's gotta get paid. And I don't make enough to cover all that and re-up."

"Chris says they're hiring down at the station."

"The radio station?"

He shook his head and said, "The police station. He says all I gotta do is fill out an application and they'll do a background check. Once I get past that, then I'll have to join the Academy. After that…" Kenny peered over at me with mischief in his eyes and said, "then I'll have a license to kill me a muthafucka."

I laughed at his foolishness. "Them white folks ain't gon' give no nigga a license to kill. You gotta have the complexion for the connection."

"Says who? I know 4 or 5 people that work for the police department, and two of them is black."

I shook my head. Clearly, he was in denial. I still had my half on the rent. It was his half that was in question. "You can think whatever you wanna think." I told him. "A man gotta draw the line somewhere. I don't see myself ever being no cop."

I may have been talking, but fate had other plans for me. A couple of nights later, someone broke into Kenny's house and robbed us at gunpoint. Kenny swore up and down the people who were responsible were my customers. I had to consider both sides of the coin. Chris and Kenny were the only ones that knew I just went to re-up. Coincidentally, that was the same night we were robbed.

"So what are you sayin'?" Kenny snarled.

"Yeah, just what are you saying?" Chris added. "Kinda sounds like you insinuating one of us may have had something with y'all gettin' robbed."

"Nah, I'm not saying that."

"Then what are you saying?" Kenny pressed on.

"I'm saying, I can't just look at things from one side. I have to look at the whole picture. Someone knew what to come in here and look for. Unless we don't figure out who that someone is, then it's just going to keep happening."

While Kenny grew visibly unsettled, Chris seemed unconcerned. "How many times you ever heard of a police officer being robbed?" Chris asked.

"Police officers don't get robbed!" Kenny said snidely.

"My point exactly," Chris insisted. "Come down to the station and fill out an application. They'll do a background check and dude, you're gonna get hired. Need I remind you a gun comes with the job if you become an officer?"

Kenny looked me square in the eye. "I say we should do it. The worst thing could happen is we get hired and stuck on desk duty."

Chris chuckled. "That'll be the day. They need guys like you to work the east side."

"What do you mean, guys like us? You sayin' they need black police officers to work the east side?"

"Precisely. I keep telling you to go down there for a reason. You think I'd be telling my best friend and his drug dealing brother to fill out an application at the police department if I didn't know something?"

No quick responses here. Where I come from, white people don't hang out with blacks, and they damn sure wouldn't help them get a job. Chris and Kenny may have been close friends, but that don't mean I had to go along with everything that came out of his mouth.

Adrian Dulan

Chapter 12
Harold

Fourteen grueling weeks had passed since the day Kenny and I joined the Police Academy. That was fourteen long weeks of giving it all that I had. The self-defense and shooting courses I took to like a fish to water. I even signed up for extra training because I wanted to be surgical with my hands.

Before I knew it, I was cruising the east side streets, just like Chris had said I would. They had me teamed up with a crazy brother named Lt. Lyons. Everyone called Lt. Lyons Nutz because of a gutsy high-speed chase he had in order to apprehend a criminal. Nutz seemed more concerned about telling me his financial problems than how to be a good cop.

"Look at all the shit we gotta do to keep this city safe," Nutz quipped. "We doing all this work for nothing. At the end of the day, I don't make enough money to pay the bills."

We'd parked at Circle K's gas station to rest for a bit. Several cars of young people crowded the parking lot. I gazed out the passenger window.

"Maybe you should try cutting back on a few things," I suggested.

"Like what? I work 10 to 12 hour shifts daily. My girlfriend keeps threatening to leave because I don't spend enough time with her. But the only reason. I don't is cause I'm always working to make extra money for her to spend."

"Then it's just like I told you. Maybe you should cut back on a few things. Stop focusing on everybody else and focus on you."

He repeated it to himself as if he were having trouble understanding. "Momma used to say that all the time. She'd say it if I put someone else's dream before my own, or if I tried to make myself out to be like someone else. But I can't see myself just up and turning my back on my girl."

"And I ain't tellin' you to do that."

"Well, if I'm not focused on her, it means I'm not focused on us. If I'm not focused on us, it means I've not only turned my back our relationship, I've turned my back on her as well."

Forget it. He was going to see things the way he wanted to. When he got tired of slavin' all those years just for someone else to squander it away, he'd dance to a new tune. Until then, ta hell with his dreams and ambitions. He needed to stay focused on his girl.

For the next couple of years, my routine was basically the same thing. Every day, Nutz and I worked the east side until it'd got to the point where I recognized names and faces. Who did what. Who started what. Who I should talk to if I needed information. As the jigsaw puzzle of how to be a better police officer came into view, so did the real reason why Chris wanted us to join the police force.

We met up one night to relax and have a couple of beers when Chris waved us all into a huddle around the table.

"Listen," Chris said. "I know it's been tough out there, but things could start to look better."

"What do you mean, could? Don't beat around the bush. Give it to me straight. It's bad enough that I feel like I've wasted two years of my life going in debt. I'm startin' to have second thoughts about wearing a badge."

Chris guzzled down half a bottle of beer and slammed the bottle on the table. He looked at each of us.

"I know you," he said. "What I'm about to stay stays strictly between us. Do we have a deal?"

I looked at Kenny, Kenny looked at Nutz, Nutz looked at Chris.

"What's the secret ?" I asked.

"Shake down," Chris spoke just above a whisper. "I say we start shakin' down local dealers. Kenny and I made a stop last week and the kid had over four fucking thousand dollars stuffed in his jeans like it wasn't nothing. Add two ounces of powder hid in the console of his car and that was easily a $10,000 stop. If I would've kept quiet and kept everything—"

"Wait a minute," Kenny interrupted. "What happened to the loyalty to the oath you swore to?"

Chris chuckled. "The only person I have loyalty to is me. If I gotta swear to get a badge that allows me to do whatever the fuck I want, so be it. I'm sick of Uncle Tom and every pencil dick son of a bitch trying to run shit up my ass."

"Shouldn't be nobody runnin' nothin' up nobody's ass," Kenny said jokingly.

"Yeah, yeah, yeah. Leave it to you to be the wise guy. My point is, I'm done getting the short end of the stick. This is free and clear money. No one is going to come asking about it." He nudged Kenny with his arm. "Nobody is going to band together with the guy that's bringing drugs into their neighborhood. This is easy money. It's ours for the taking. If we all stick together, nothing can stop us!"

Obviously, we had to consider what Chris planned to start doing. Kenny's eyes roamed around the room. The bar was quiet that night. Nutz bobbed his head to a song he remembered. That's what he did when he was in deep thought.

"What exactly do we gotta do to get this free money?" I asked. "Are people gonna get hurt?"

Chris waved his hands in the air. "No, no, no!" he exclaimed. "Only if we have to. We're actually doing the bad guys a favor."

"And how you figure that?"

"Prison for ten years, or hand over your dope." He shrugged. "Go figure. Look, guys, it gets no easier than this. By now, we all know who the dealers and pushers are. Now, it's time to tax their asses. Can somebody please tell me: who's gonna come downtown and report a police officer that had stolen their dope?"

No one said a word. He took a beer from a bucket and popped the top. He held the bottle up. One by one, each of us took a bottle from the bucket, popped the top, then we toasted.

A few days later, Nutz and I were on the prowl for our first victim. Nutz hit the lights on a blue station wagon. The car pulled over. I stood next to the passenger window while Nutz spoke with the driver.

"License and registration," Nutz said.

The driver, a young teen, reached to get them out of the glove box, but Nutz wasn't having it. "You keep your gotdamn hands where I can see 'em!"

The young teen froze. "You told me to get my license and registration."

"I told you to keep yo' gotdamn hands where I can. see 'em." Nutz shined his flashlight inside the car. The floor was covered in trash. Amongst the empty McDonalds bags and empty cups, a bottle peeked from beneath. I hit my flashlight. A joint stuck out of the ashtray.

"I clocked you doin' 37 in a 35," Nutz said.

"That's only two miles over the speed limit."

"Shut your damn mouth! You don't speak unless spoken to. You don't think we know how many miles over the speed limit you were going?"

"No, I was just—"

"'Bout to get high," I said, completing his sentence. I shined my light on the ashtray.

"You sneaky son of a bitch," Nutz seethed. He opened the door and snatched the driver out by the shirt. "I think we got ourselves a real live drug dealer, here. What do you got to say about that, Officer Dunlap?"

I dug around under the passenger's seat and found a brand-new bottle of Mad Dog 20/20. I fished around some more. Lighter, cigarette butts, coins, and a quarter sack of week. "I say he's lookin' at 5 to 10 easily." I held up the weed and bottle of liquor. "An open container can get you——"

"That bottle is brand new!" the young teen insisted. " I hadn't even had time to open it."

I twisted the lid off the bottle and drank from it. Reminded me of Fruit Punch Kool-Aid. I held the bottle out for Nutz.

"Don't mind if I do," he said. After Nutz took a sip, we both stood glaring down at the young teen.

"Now, it's your turn."

The driver looked as if he couldn't believe what I'd just told him to do. He sipped from the bottle and passed it back. I put the lid back on.

"So, if you didn't have time to open this bottle of liquor, when did the bottle get opened?" I held the bottle up for him to see that it had been open.

Suddenly, the driver must have realized he was in a no-win situation. Nutz cuffed him and spun him around to face his car.

"I don't wanna go to jail," he cried. "I'll do anything, just please don't lock me up."

Nutz and I looked at each other at the same time. This was our guy.

That one stop was the beginning of a string of shake downs. Cocky dealers we caught red-handed, we not only emptied their pockets, we stripped them of their car stereo, jewelry, any brand name items. If it was worth any money, we took it. Before long, people got hip to what type of time we were on. They didn't know if we were there to plant something, take something, or frame someone. All they knew to do was give us what we wanted. We had every Tom, Dick, and Harry this side of the Cimarron River shaking in their boots. But with fear came caution. Cats got smart and started working together. We had to be creative if we planned to continue to make money.

Nutz knew a couple of girls that worked at Circle J's Gas Station. Every now and then we'd stop by before out shift was over, whenever we went inside, the cashier would always give me a peculiar look. She was an attractive dark-skinned woman, but I knew she was Nutz's girl, and that's why I never really paid her attention.

While I busied myself flipping through a magazine, Nutz talked to the cashier.

"What time you supposed to be gettin' off work?" he asked her.

"Why? It ain't like you really care," she sassed him. "You ask me that same stupid question every time you come in here."

"You think I'd be askin' if I hadn't made plans to come and see you?"

A woman cleared her throat in a manner to get everyone's attention. We all looked in her direction. "I thought you was supposed to be introducing me to this fine young gentleman."

The cashier gave me another funny look and asked, "Babe, what's your friend's name?"

Nutz looked over at me with a raised eyebrow. "Ask him yourself," he replied sarcastically. "If a man got a mouth, then he got a name."

"Officer Dunlap," I said, trying to ease the suspense.

"Well, Officer Dunlap, this is Shela. Shela, this is Officer Dunlap. There. Are you satisfied? I introduced y'all."

While Nutz and the lady at the register continued to talk, Shela sauntered over from the Hot Food section. From what I could tell, she was much older than me. Possibly 7 to 10 years older. She was a healthy woman. A blond woman. She wore very little makeup with her hair in a bun. The only thing attractive about her was her breasts. They were plump, just the way I liked them.

"What's it gonna take for a girl like me to hook up with a guy like you?"

I chuckled. "From what I hear, Nutz is supposed to be pickin' your friend up tonight. Maybe we could hang out then."

Shela glared at Nutz and said. "Yeah, he always says that, but tonight he's really gonna come back, ain't chu', Nutz?"

He looked back at her and rolled his eyes as she strolled back over to her work area.

Later that night, we took the girls back to Kenny's house to chill. Since neither of the girls had a friend Kenny could hang out with, he joined in on a few drinks before retiring to his bedroom for the night.

Nutz broke out a bottle of tequila and three shot glasses. "How 'bout a game of Truth or Dare?" he asked.

The girls seemingly grew excited.

"I wanna ask the first question." Shela said. "Truth or Dare?" she asked me.

"Truth."

She thought about a good question she could ask. "You ain't never been with a white woman before, have you?"

I guess that must've been obvious, cause everyone burst into laughter while Nutz handed me a shot glass. Little did Shela know she'd just opened the door for the game to go to the next level.

Now it was my turn. "Truth, or Dare?" I asked Shela.

"Dare." She replied with no fear.

"I dare you to show us one good reason why I should've been with a white woman."

Shela and I sat on the loveseat across from Nutz and Kathy on the sofa. Shela wiggled her dress around until she managed to lift it to her waist. She hiked her leg over the arm of the chair. Her feminine folds nearly swallowed the crotch of her pink panties. "That good enough reason for you?" she said.

My mouth fell wide open. That was the prettiest, pinkest chunk of pussy I done ever seen in my life. That a good enough reason. That was the absolute correct answer. I was so mesmerized at the sight of it, my mouth started watering. I wanted to smell it. I leaned closer. She giggled. It didn't smell.

"Nah, uh-uh!" Kathy quipped. She hopped up and all but snatched my face away from her crouch. "Are we gonna finish playing the game, or what? We just got started and y'all already tryin' to be nasty."

Nutz peered over Kathy's shoulder and said, "Nigga, damn what she talkin' 'bout. I wanna see you do it."

I was borderline in shock, borderline drooling. I wanted to kiss on that big pretty muthafucka. Fuck it.

Whap! Kathy slapped me.

"What in the hell is wrong with you?" I snarled.

Nutz looked on, dumbfounded, with one hand covering his mouth. Shela snickered as she pulled her dress back over her legs.

"Oops, I'm sorry," Kathy said. "That was an accident. I was just trying to grab you. Your face must've fell into my hand."

"That look like some flat-out cock blockin'," Nutz said. "Let the man go and eat him some pussy. Man been workin' all day, he gotta eat."

Although the game continued on, my mind was still stuck on what I just saw. Shela might not have been much of a sight to look at, but her pussy made up the difference. Kathy may have been cock blockin', but there was always a way around a hater.

"What do you say you and me go back to my room?"

Shela scoffed. She tugged at her black blazer as if she didn't want to be bothered. "Doesn't make sense to," she replied. "If we just gon' go back there and talk, we can do that in here." In so many words, that was her way of saying she wanted me to hit it.

Since Kathy didn't like the smell of reefer, I used that as an excuse for Shela and I to go in my bedroom. I led Shela in my room and closed the door behind us. She sat on the foot of the bed and relaxed.

"My back has been killing me for the last few weeks," she said. "Every day I'm on my feet and I know that can't be no good for me." She scooted further back on the bed and leaned back on her elbow.

I rested my hand on her thigh. "I'm pretty good at fixin' back problems." I explained.

Her eyes narrowed and she lit a cigarette. "Everyone says that."

"Well, I ain't everybody." I leaned in and tried to kiss her.

She stopped. "I know what you want," she said.

"Then why you stallin'? You know your crazy-ass friend fixin' to be bangin' on that door any second."

She lay back and slid the shoulder straps over her arms. I lifted her dress and massaged the camel toe that had drenched her panties. I moved them to the side, ran my fingers over her clit. She moaned. She grabbed my hand and sucked the juice off of them.

Quickly, I unbuckled my jeans and climbed on top of her. "Wait," she panted lustfully. "Do you have protection?" I tried to stick it in. She brushed it away. She covered her pussy with her hand. "You've got to have a condom."

"I thought you wanted to come in here and get busy," I spoke in her ear. My dick slid over her hand and leg. I managed to move her fingers some. She let me stick the tip in.

She gasped. "Harold." I pumped a few times. Each stroke, she let me get deeper and deeper. "Wait. You don't understand."

Too late. I was all the way in her.

Clop! Clop! Clop! Clop! Clop!

With each toe-curling thrust, she fought desperately not to scream. She even went so far as to suck on my neck to keep from screaming. "Uhhh!"

I covered her mouth and said, "You can't be doin' that. They think we back here smokin', not fucking. You think you gon' be able to handle this dick quietly?" I kissed her on the cheek and grinded deep inside of her. I held it.

It was a test. She sneered. She passed.

Clop! Clop! Clop!

Left angle. Right angle. Long-stroked it. We both watched as her juices covered my shaft. Her moaning and groaning got to be so loud I was forced to stop again.

"You must want me to go back up front," I whispered to her. "All that noise is gon' make your nosy-ass friend come back here."

Shela peered up at me pleadingly. "Don't stop," she said. "I'm about to cum." She ground up into me. I felt her walls caving in. I pinned her legs back as far as they would go and pounded relentlessly.

Clop! Clop! Clop! Clop! Clop! Clop! Clop!

Her titties bounced as I pounced. I kept pounding, switching angles, pounding, switching angles. Every time my dick came out of her, it was whiter than it was before.

Clop! Clop! Clop! Clop! Clop!

She was begging and pleading in a low tone. The more she tried to get away from me, the harder I clamped down. When I finally began to feel my dick swell, I pulled out and shot nut all over her stomach.

Not long after we finished up, Kathy called for Shela. "Y'all ain't done smokin', yet?"

We straightened our clothes as best as we could, just as Kathy barged in my room. "What's taking y'all so—" She paused. "What in the world is that smell?"

Shela quickly lit a cigarette to try and cover up the odor. "Maybe it's that fire Harold gave me to smoke," she said. "He got that real skunk weed, not that homegrown stuff that these boys be runnin' round here sellin'."

"If you ask me, it smells more like a dead skunk," Kathy quipped. "Anything that smells like that can't be good for you. So, now that y'all are done, come back up front so we can finish the game."

Chapter 13
Harold

The next morning, I was awakened by Kathy rummaging through her purse. "Lord Jesus," she hissed softly. "If I find out that bitch done left with my—" She shook her head and sighed. "Lord, forgive me."

"Can't you see I'm over here trying to get some sleep?" I said. "It's bad enough you slapped me in the face last night. Now, you wanna wake me up with all this noise."

She lifted the pillows on the sofa, searching. Nothing. She shuffled their clothes around on the floor. Still nothing. Her eyes roamed over every inch of the carpet, and that's when I noticed it. Shela was gone. Kenny was gone too. His bedroom door stood wide open. Nutz was sound asleep on the floor.

"Either someone done stole my stuff, or someone got it," Kathy snarled. "My shit didn't just up and disappear on its own."

"Just because you lost something, don't mean wake everyone up in the damn house!"

She glared at me as if I were the cause of her dilemma. "Does it look like everybody in the house is woke?" She got down on all fours and looked under the sofa. The fact that she only wore pink panties and a long white T-shirt bought her more time to look. I guess whatever she'd been looking for, she must've found it. She held up a small plastic bag and thumped it.

"Is that what all the fuss is about?" I asked her.

"Sure is. You wanna try some?" She poured a small pile of white powder on the coffee table.

Doing drugs had never been my cup of tea. As far as I'd known, it had never been Nutz's thing either. Being a police officer required us to take random urine analysis. Course, Kathy wouldn't know nothing about that. She was a cashier at a gas station. She was at the height of her career.

She quickly made two lines of powder and snorted them through a dollar bill that had been made into a straw. She swiped at her nose and pinched it. "Now, it's your turn."

I know I had to be looking at her like she'd lost her mind.

"What?" she asked. "You scared to get——" She paused, looking as if she'd suddenly thought of something. "You've never tried cocaine before, have you?"

"Duhhh. I'm a cop. How many cops you know sneaking around shovin' this mess up their nose?"

"You'd be surprised."

I snatched the straw out of her hand and snorted both lines just as quickly as she had. When I was done, I did what she did. I brushed at my nose and pinched it. Disgusting, I thought.

"How was it?" Kathy asked.

"What?"

"Do you like it? That's probably the best coke you'll find anywhere in the city. Ain't a lotta people done had the chance to try it. I guess you could say you're one of the lucky ones."

At first, I was like, big fucking deal. What was so special about cocaine? I felt the exact same way I did when I woke up that morning. Mad. Outside of the sting I felt when I first snorted that stuff, nothing felt different.

Then it hit me.

Little by little, the sound in the house was fading out. My ears started ringing. I looked around the living room. Kathy started to say something, but I stopped her.

"Shhh!" I held one finger to my lips. "You don't hear that shit?"

A small dog barked feverishly. Its claws clawed at the bathroom door. It was trapped - three blocks over, the third house from the corner.

I was tripping.

I got up and went to wash my face. Maybe some cold water against my face would make me feel normal again. The ringing hadn't stopped. My nuts started tingling. I had to piss. Quickly, I rushed over to the toilet and unzipped my jeans. "Oh—my—God!" My dick ain't never been this big. My shit had some extra length, thickness. I wanted to show the world what cocaine had done for me.

I strolled back in the living room feeling like the coolest mutha-fucka on the planet. Couldn't nobody tell me nothing. I was that guy. Kathy was still seated at the coffee table, which was right where I'd left her. The only bad part about that was, I had a bigger dick. I had a bigger dick and she was half-naked. Wasn't no way I was supposed to feel comfortable around my partner's half-naked girlfriend. Mind you, Kathy wasn't no ugly woman. She might have been a little flirtatious, but that was somebody else's problem to deal with.

As the morning drifted away in to the sunny afternoon, we carried our coke snorting festivities into the kitchen. Kathy made breakfast while I sat at the dining room table snorting powder. Occasionally, Kathy would saunter past my chair, but intentionally bump me with her hip. Soon her intentional brush against me was met by my own aggressive response. I had to show the world what cocaine had done for me.

I grabbed her by the waist and snatched her back to me. "You ain't gon' stop until I get a hold of you, huh?

She laughed and replied, "Looks like you've already got me." She turned so that her breast was resting against my face. Her nipples were already hard. I couldn't do this to my partner.

"What, you scared of pussy too?" she asked.

"Nutz is gon' go crazy if he wake up and see us doin' it."

"Sound like to me, you more worried about some other nigga, than all this woman you got in your face."

That was it. I spun her ass around and quickly moved her panties to the side.

"Wait!" she said.

"For what? You was talkin' all that noise. Now I'm ready to get busy."

She looked as if she didn't want to say. "Did you fuck Shela last night?"

"The hell type of question is that?" I slid my dick down between her ass cheeks, guiding it to her pussy.

She moved. "Just answer the question," she said.

"Hell nah, I ain't fuck that bitch. Did you fuck Nutz?"

She knew better than to try and lie about that. She knew damn well I saw her riding him in the wee hours of the morning. Just the thought of what I saw made me put her on her tiptoes.

"Sssss," she hissed.

I couldn't fuck her the way I wanted to, but I damn sho' fucked her the way she needed me to. I covered her mouth with my hand and ran every inch of me inside of her.

As the day carried on into the evening, what had been done in the dark came to the light. The swelling I'd noticed in my penis was from a severe case of gonorrhea. I was burning like a wildfire in California. I'd scorched every thing I'd touched. Since Nutz didn't know that I'd slept with Kathy, guess what? Sizzle. Burned his ass too. Kenny may have thought he was being slick by running off with Shela. Guess what? She lit his ass up, too. Once we all put the pieces of the puzzle together of how this could have happened, all signs lead back to Shela.

"Funky bitch."

"You fucked her!" Kathy spat.

"So? You fucked Nutz right there on the living room floor."

"I asked you if you'd fucked her and you stood there and lied to my face."

"I tol' yo' scandalous ass what you wanted to hear. Besides, you wasn't gon' leave me alone until I got a hold of you."

"I asked you for a reason, Harold," Kathy said, sounding defeated. "I would've told you she had an STD."

I looked all upside her head. "Well, if you knew the bitch was burnin', then why the hell did you hook us up? You just as wrong as she is."

The euphoria cocaine gave me was unlike any feeling I'd ever felt. Soon, I longed for that feeling night and day. The worst part about it was, I had to go through Kathy if I wanted the best dope in the city. But to go through her meant there was one more nostril to powder.

Kenny was a lot like me when it came to doing drugs. He was skeptical at first, but when he got his first taste, he got sucked in just like the rest of us. We started doing stupid shit to support our addiction.

Naturally, it wasn't long before word reached the captain's ears about how far out there we'd gotten. He called us into his office one morning as soon as we arrived at work.

"Gentlemen, have a seat," the captain said while he flipped through the contents of a file. "We've been getting a lotta complaints sayin' you boys are involved in all sorts of illegal activities. Would either of you care to shed some light on what I've been hearing?"

Nutz looked at me. I looked at Kenny. Kenny looked at Chris. No one said a word.

There was a knock at the door.

"Come in!" the captain shouted. Two men from the Internal Affairs Office came in and flanked both sides of the captain's chair. "I've asked that these men open an investigation on these allegations."

"Investigation? But you haven't said anything about what we were supposed to had done."

He chuckled. "Supposed to *have*? I find that hard to believe." He thumbed through several pages until he found what he'd been looking for. "Says here, on October 5th, Lt. Lyons and Officer Dunlap stopped a blue station wagon for speeding." He paused and peered over the top of his glasses. "Any of this ring a bell?"

"Cap, we've stopped countless people since then," Lt. Lyons said. "What does us making a stop have to do with being investigated?"

"Hold your horses. I was just gettin' to the good part. The report goes on to say you and Mr. Dunlap here let the driver leave with a warning?"

Lt. Lyons shrugged. "Is that a crime?"

The Captain smiled. "What about the open container?"

"What open container?"

"The one you opened and made him drink."

Nutz looked at me as if it were my turn to take the wheel. Hell, I figured he'd been doin' a fine job on his own. He didn't need me to say something and blow this thing wide open in our face.

"I didn't open nothin' and make anyone drink a damn thing!" Nutz clarified.

"That's not what these fellas seem to think. They say they've got evidence that you and Mr. Dunlap been settin' folks up on bogus stops, just so you could rob 'em."

"Cap' I swear on the Holy Bible—"

The captain held up one hand, silencing him, and said, "Don't even bother. The two of you tested dirty for cocaine. The community don't need the likes of you patrolling there streets. I'm going to allow you to pick from one of two options. Either turn in your gun and badge and walk away from this thing as free men, or I'll turn this file over to these gentlemen and they can take it from there."

For me, my mind was already made up what I'd do as soon as he'd said it. I couldn't care less about being a police officer in the first place. I made a hell of a lot more money selling pills than I did punchin' a clock. Luckily, Internal Affairs didn't have a case on Kenny and Chris. They simply had them sit on our meeting so they'd see what happened to us, because word was starting to circulate about them as well.

Chapter 14
Harold

"So— what are we gonna do now?" Kenny asked. He, too, had resigned from the police department when I did. Once word got around that he was suspected of being a dirty cop, the only job available was desk duty.

"We gon' keep right on doin' what we been doin'," I insisted. "One wrong turn don't mean we should cancel the trip. We done came too far to turn back, now. The mission is to get money."

"I wish it could be that easy," Kenny said. "Brothers been lookin' all upside my head every time I go to the store."

"Fuck them negros! Don't nobody know we resigned."

"But who's to say they won't find out? When people catch wind of why we had to resign..." He paused as if at a loss for words. "There's gonna be trouble. Brothers is gon' be lookin' to get even."

"The only thing they gon' look and find is a bullet right between the eyes. That's why all of us got to stick together and make sure we're on the same page."

Kenny looked slightly confused. "Same page to do what?"

"To keep doin' what we've been doin'. We've all got habits, don't we?" He nodded. "We all still got bills to pay, right?" He nodded again.

"But you ain't makin' no sense, Harold. How we gonna keep shakin' folks down and we don't have a uniform or a badge?"

"Folks is plural. I'm talkin' 'bout one muthafucka. In and out. Cash on deck. And what makes this shakedown so finger lickin' good is that nobody will know a thing. Everything is planned out. Once we get everyone together, we'll go over the details.

In the weeks that followed, Kathy and I grew closer. After I got gonorrhea from Shela and gave it to Kathy, she gave it to Nutz. Nutz, unknowingly, gave his main squeeze the STD and the rest was history. His girl sent him packing.

Kathy became our only means to score cocaine. Course, we couldn't afford to let her get too far away. Not only was she our only means to purchase drugs; she was also the bait we used to set people up. Throw in a scandalous STD-packin' white bitch, and the money kept rolling in as if we'd never resigned.

As time would tell, Kathy dated an eastside gangster by the name of Fast Eddy. Honestly, I think their relationship was something she'd made up in her head. Fast Eddy still dated several other women, yet somehow Kathy claimed he'd cheated on her. Whatever the case was between them, Fast Eddy was our ticket to a large supply of coke. We had Kathy to keep a close eye on his whereabouts, that way we knew what we were runnin' in to.

Usually, Fast Eddy worked from his small hole in the wall bar. If he wasn't there, he'd be conducting business out of the Metro Apartments. The complex sat just off I-35 and NE 23rd. It was built like a fortress with a huge steel gate around the property. Outside of the apartment security waiting at the front gate, Fast Eddy had two foot soldiers nearby on the lookout for anything suspicious. We came up with codes that the security guards Kathy had paid would let us through.

"Apartment 564," Kenny said. He'd pulled up to the guard shack at the front gate. The guard looked at him skeptically then leaned down to peer inside the car. "I'm gonna need to see some ID," he said. "Been a lotta knuckle heads trying to get in here. We doin' everything we can to keep things peaceful tonight."

"Can't you just buzz apartment 564 and tell Pam that we're here?"

The guard's eyes lit up. Apartment 564 was just a number we threw out there. Pam was the code to let us in.

Kenny drove around to apartment 222 and parked. Unlike the other buildings, the building that housed apartment 222 only had two people living there. Although Fast Eddy didn't know Kenny or me, we still needed to make sure very few people saw us.

Kenny and I strolled up to the apartment, but noticed the curtain upstairs was partially open.

Moments later, we were inside. The apartment was cluttered with boxes stacked on top of each other, as if someone was moving. Luckily, Kathy told us right where to look. The kitchen stove was made to look as if it worked, but it didn't. We pulled it out and re-moved the money that had been hidden in the wall.

When we got everything back to the house, Chris and Nutz met up with us to divide the spoils.

"$156,000," I informed everyone. "That's enough dough to move to California and never come back."

Kathy had a pile of coke on a plate where she split the dope five ways. "Nobody leaves and goes nowhere," Kathy said. "If people start leavin' town, it's gonna be a dead giveaway that we're the ones responsible for stealin' his shit."

Kenny scoffed. "Your man don't know us, no more than he know Santa Claus. We ain't got no reason to stick around. We could use this money and start a whole new life."

"We agreed on what we'd do before we done this," Chris chimed in.

"We?" I repeated skeptically. "Muthafucka, you ain't done shit. All you did was sit back and watch while we done all the work. To be straight up, I don't think you deserve a dime of this money. We done the work, so we should get the money."

"If Eddy and his hardcore friends every find out what y'all done, then what? Y'all got a plan for that?" Nutz asked.

Kenny looked to me as if I were actually about to say something logical. Instead, I set my snub nose 38. on the table and said, "That a good enough plan for you? I bet once this babe gets to knockin' chunks out his ass, they won't be callin' him Fast Eddy no mo'. That nigga will be Dead Eddy."

Chris chuckled forcefully. "That's only one gun. You gon' need at least ten more. Besides, we started this thing together, so we'll end it together. If this whole thing goes sour, you can always count on me."

As much as I didn't want to believe him, I had to.

Before sunset, the decision was made to stick close and watch each other's backs. Kathy decided to move in with us for a bit. She didn't feel comfortable being alone, not knowing if Fast Eddy sus-pected her as being the cause of his shit comin' up missing. People were known to disappear for far less things than what we done.

The DA's office had several pending investigations against Fast Eddy, but nothing that would stick.

While we spent the next several weeks off the radar, word got around that Kenny and I were responsible for what happened to Fast Eddy's stuff. Shela called Kathy one morning, crying hysterically.

"Calm down," Kathy consoled Shela. "Stop crying and tell me exactly what they said, starting from the beginning." Kathy listened intently while Shela explained what happened. Every now and then she'd sigh and shake her head.

Click.

She hung up.

"Here's the deal," Kathy began by saying. "Someone saw Kenny's car the night y'all went to Eddy's place."

Kenny got up and came in the kitchen and sat across from me at the dining room table. "Bullshit!" he snarled. "No one saw us pull up to that apartment. It was dark and there was a whole lotta people out that night. Plus, we ain't do nothing to draw any attention."

"Maybe one of his workers must've realized we wasn't from around there," I tried to reason. "I noticed the funny looks they was given us as we drove through the gates."

"So, what are we gonna do?" Kathy asked. "Sooner or later Eddy's gonna come lookin' for his money. Instead of worrying about who saw what, we need to grab whatever we can and get outta here!"

"I wish the hell I would. Just because that STD-packin' bitch done got scared don't mean I'm fixin' to let it rub off on me."

Kathy hurried into the living room and started grabbing her things. "I've known Shela for over ten years," Kathy said. "One thing she won't do is lie to me about this. I could hear it in her voice. She was scared to death."

"And? What does that got to do with us? It ain't my fault her stupid ass is still working at that damn gas station. Ain't that right, Kenny?"

He got up and went to look out the window. Agnew was a busy street any time of the day or night. The constant traffic made it difficult to spot someone watching our home.

"I think you've got a point," Kenny said to me as he went and sat down on the sofa. "If Fast Eddy was as hardcore as they say he is, then why ain't Shela dead? Why he ain't showed up here demanding that we hand over his money?"

Kathy dragged her suitcases in the living room, seemingly oblivious to our conversation.

Finally, I'd had enough. "Put that shit down!" I snapped at Kathy, startling her. She stood in the doorway to my bedroom with tears in her eyes. "You're overreacting. Just because Shela supposedly heard something doesn't mean it's true. And even if it is, we got someone on our side that works for the police. They better not come half-steppin'. In fact... Kenny, call Chris and find out what we should do."

For the next half hour, Kenny called Chris repeatedly, only to get no answer. Surprisingly, we got the same result when we called Nutz. Kathy came up with the idea to stop by his sister's house, which was where he'd been staying.

Kenny rang the doorbell and we waited patiently. Kathy waited in the car. Across the street, someone cranked up a lawn mower. It was a little boy. He gave me the finger. I gave him one right back.

"You think they're asleep?" I inquired. "His car is right there in the driveway. His sister, who is much older than him, almost always at home."

Kenny tried to look through the front window, but the curtains had been closed. "When have you known Nutz to be asleep in the middle of the day?" Kenny replied. "I say we check around back. Make sure it ain't been no funny business. Something about this whole thing don t feel right."

We went to the side of the house and through the back gate. Nutz's sister's house was in a prestigious neighborhood. It was two blocks away from the State Capitol. This was an uncommon area for any mischief.

The sliding glass door was open when we arrived at the patio. I drew my weapon.

"Put that thing away!" Kenny hissed. "If someone sees you with that thing, they're gonna think we're up to no good."

Course, I couldn't care less what someone else thought of me. My gun was for my safety.

Kenny opened the glass door some more and we went inside. "Nutz, you in here?"

The television was on, which made me that much more suspicious that something wasn't right. Several broken plates were scattered about the dining room and kitchen floor.

"It looks like something happened." I cocked the hammer back on my gun and Kenny allowed me to take the lead.

First, we checked the bathroom. Same thing. Broken. objects lay scattered about the floor. Just as I turned to inspect the rest of the house, Kenny stopped me.

"Look!" Blood was smeared down the hall leading to the garage. "I think we oughta get outta here."

I wasn't leaving until I had answers. I couldn't live comfortably knowing someone was out to kill me. I suppose that's how Shela felt.

I carefully opened the door to Nutz's sister's room. Her dresser drawers had been emptied and tossed around the room. We quickly moved on to the next room, and the next, until finally, we made it to the garage. When I opened the door, my worst fears became a reality.

"They're dead," I said to Kenny. "Someone must've came in and killed them recently. Shela was right. Eddy has been lookin' for us."

Nutz's sister was face down on the concrete. Someone had shot her in the back of the head. The hole was so big that part of her brain had oozed out onto the concrete. I went over to check Nutz. Dead as a doorknob. He'd been tied to a chair with a plastic bag placed over his head. A knife had been shoved down his throat.

We quickly back tracked through the house and back out to the car. Kathy sat in the back seat nervously awaiting our report.

"So what happened?" she asked.

"They're dead."

"Who?"

"Nutz and his sister!"

"Oh my God. Oh my God! We need to stop and get Shela." Kathy insisted.

"Fuck Shela. I say we go back to the house and get the rest of our money. We can get a plane ticket out——"

"We're not leaving Shela!"

"The hell if we ain't!" Kenny started the car and backed out of the driveway.

The neighbor waved as they watered the lawn. We all waved back.

"If we ain't three of the dumbest people alive?" I snarled. "We all goin' to jail."

Kenny spared a peek at me as he drove.

"The hell is you talkin' about, Harold? If you wanna go to prison, then be my guest. I don't need no one speakin' negativity into my life." He stepped on the gas.

"Look, all I'm saying is, we just waved at the fuckin' neighbors. That means someone saw" us leave the scene of a crime."

Understanding must've finally registered. Kenny's mouth hung wide open.

"Slow this damn thing down!" Kathy squealed. "If Eddy don't get us, the cops sure as hell will."

Kenny slowed down until we were cruising, doing the speed limit. "What do y'all think we should do?" Kenny inquired while on the verge of panic.

"I think everyone needs to chill the fuck out and let me think. When the police discover those bodies, they're gonna want answers. We've gotta be ready for that. The chief already suspects us of being a bunch of dirty cops. The logical thing to do is pick up Shela, and get outta town. By the time detectives start snoopin' around, we will be long gone."

Shela lived in a two-bedroom duplex not far from her job. The area was overrun with drug dealers and gang members that we'd shook down on numerous occasions. Luckily, no one recognized Kenny's car when we pulled up. A few people gave us cold stares as we went to the door. It was open.

"Fuck, fuck, fuck, fuuuck!" We spun around and made a beeline back to the car and got in.

"What happened?" Kathy asked, trying to make sense of why we had returned to the car without going in.

"They got her."

"You saw her?'

"I saw enough to know that bitch is dead."

Kathy opened the back door and got out. "I'm not leaving without her," she snarled.

"Then I'll see you on the other side."

Kenny sat staring in a daze at Shela's place. "We can't leave her," he admitted grudgingly.

"I don't see why not. All you gotta do is put the car in reverse and drive the fuck off."

Kenny got out as well. "We need to make sure there's no one else that knows what we done," he said. "If she's in there, I'm here to get her. If she's dead, we don't have to worry about her ever turning on us."

Since I was the only one with a gun, I took the lead. Kathy refused to wait in the car, so she trailed close behind Kenny. When we walked inside, Shela's place was just like Nutz's sister's house. Broken items lay everywhere. Kenny gave me a knowing look. We both knew what we'd find.

Kathy screamed. "Ahhh!"

Sheal had been tied to her bed naked. She'd been cut open from her feminine folds to her breasts. Her intestines laid exposed for all to see.

"Satisfied?" I asked as they looked on in utter disbelief. "They'll probably be comin' for us next. Y'all tryin' to stick around and see what he's got planned to do to us? Or should we get the rest of our things and get the hell out of town?"

The latter was our only option. From the looks of things, Fast Eddy wasn't working with a full deck.

We shot straight back to Kenny's crib to pack our things. Kathy already had most of her clothes packed. She finished packing in no time, then helped Kenny carry our things out to the car.

I grabbed everything I could and dumped it in a duffle bag. When I heard several car doors slam, I paused.

"Kenny?"

Maybe Kenny just slammed the trunk, I thought. Kathy could've closed the door. Kenny could've too. I grabbed another drawer and was on the verge of dumping it, then I thought about something. Where the hell was everyone at?

I grabbed my strap and went to see what was going on. A yellow Cadillac Coupe Deville was parked in the driveway behind Kenny's car. A white '98 Oldsmobile was parked on the curve. A van was parked behind it. Kenny and Kathy were inside.

"I was wondering how long it'd take before you brought yo' ass outta there," a man said. He leaned against the hood of the Cadillac in the driveway. He wore a red and white Troop sweat suit with fat gold ropes around his neck.

"Do I know you from somewhere? I think there's been some kind of mistake."

He chuckled forcefully. "Mistake, indeed. Seems to me you and those two over there have something that belongs to me."

I looked at Kenny and he started to cry. A man wearing a Kango held a gauge to his head. Kathy wept uncontrollably. She tried to hide her face, but couldn't.

"Listen, me and my brother are officers of the law."

"You mean you *were* officers of the law," the man clarified. "Y'all ain't nothin' but a bunch of junkies doin' whateva it takes to get high. Being that time is money and money is time, I'm going to give you one chance to tell me where my shit is at. If you lie, I'm gonna do you just like I did Shela and your friend, Nutz." He removed a hunting knife from under his jacket and began cleaning his fingernails.

"If I tell you where the money is, will you let us go?"

"You and your brother, yes. But that backstabbin' bitch of mine has got to pay. I plan to get medieval on her ass. And when the bitch dies, I'm gon' resurrect her ass and kill her again."

"The rest of what I have is in the trunk."

"The rest?" Fast Eddy repeated mockingly. "You said that like you spent up a nice chunk of my money."

"I only spent two grand in the last couple of weeks. Whatever I don't have, I'll pay you back."

"With interest," he insisted.

"With interest," I agreed.

"What about what they stole?" he went on to inquire about. "How you plan to square up on that?"

"I guess we'll have to put our heads together and figure this thing out."

Fast Eddy sent one of his men to get his money out of the trunk. Once he'd found what he was looking for, Fast Eddy ordered his men to release Kenny.

"Let him go!" he barked.

Kenny fell to his knees on the lawn and vomited.

Fast Eddy strolled up to me on the porch and said, "You've got one week to make a payment on what you owe me."

"But you never said how much we supposed to give you."

"25 large."

"$25,000 ? I only spent a couple of thousand."

"And so did Kenny. And let's not forget about Nutz. And what about Shela? Add all that together, plus my fees and interest, comes out to $27,253.17."

"But you just said—"

"$28,000."

"Are you cra-"

"$31,000, and I can keep going up the longer you put up a fuss. The only reason I'm lettin' you walk away from this is because my connect is your brother."

I didn't understand. "Baby Leonard?"

"That's what I said, ain't it? Besides, why you call that fool, Baby Leonard when he is a stone cold killa?"

"To me, he's just my little brother. This talk about him being a stone cold killa is news to my ears."

"Well, here's some more news you can use. You've got one week to pay on what you owe me. If you don't have my money, I suggest you pursued that baby brother of yours to come down on his prices for me."

With that said, Fast Eddy and his crew left. Had we never got in the business of shakin' folks down, this mess wouldn't be happening all these years later. The best thing I could think to do was talk to Cabbage and try to dead this madness before it got out of hand.

Chapter 15
Kevin

Fireworks lit up the sky as H.E.R. whaled away at her guitar. Suddenly, the lights went out. The crowd roared with excitement as the drummer hammered at his drum set.

Josilin swirled her hips to the beat while dancing in front of me. "You're mine," she said and winked. We kissed.

The longer the song played, the more I understood. That very day, that very moment, the lights, the crowd, the music was all for me.

We made It.

I was half a million dollars richer. Muthafuck the feds and the DA. I hit my quarter and I was out. Done. It was time for me to put the streets in my rearview.

"You ready?" Josilin asked.

I checked my watch. It was late. Downtown Oklahoma City was already packed before the concert began. If I didn't want to be stuck for an hour just to get out of the parking lot, we'd best get going.

"I'm driving this time," I told her. "I wanna feel them lips kissing all over me before I drop you off at the crib."

Josilin looked at me, puzzled. "You're not stayin' the night?" she inquired.

That was my cue. I took her by the hand and headed down the aisle. Date nights were her night. Any other day of the week, I could do me. Josilin knew about LaShura, our family, everything. All she wanted was one day out of the week.

"Why haven't you said something?" she said.

We'd made it out to the parking lot and got in the car.

"Why haven't I said something about what? We've been talking the entire time on the way out to the car."

"Yeah, but you never answered my question."

"Which was?"

"Are you staying the night? Earlier, you said you wanted to feel—"

"Yeah, yeah, yeah. I know what I said." I started the car and pulled into traffic.

"Then you remember that you said—"

"I told you, I know what I said, Josilin."

"You promised me that date night was our night."

"But that was before all this shit went down."

"All this shit?" she repeated mockingly. "It's been shit goin' down ever since we met! If I would've listened to Nancy——"

"Fuck Nancy!"

"I'm sure she feels the same way about you."

"Josilin, let's not do this right now. We just had a good time at the concert. Let's not end this on a sour note."

"You're saying that as if this is my fault."

"No, I'm saying it so that this doesn't turn into an argument."

"Why would there be an argument?" she pressed on. "You gave me your word."

"But that was before we hit that last lick."

She laughed. "Speaking of licks - I rented the car you were in. I helped you. If anyone saw your license plate, those people you robbed are gonna come lookin' for me!"

I sighed. "Josilin, please. You don't even know what you're talking about. Are you still alive?"

She scoffed and turned to peer out into the night. "Sometimes I think you think our relationship is a game."

"Don't try to switch this around and turn it into something else. I asked you a simple question and the answer is obvious. Yes, you're still alive. If those people had my tag number, we would've already been dead." I pulled in front of her house and waited for her to get out.

"It's like that?" she asked.

"Don't start this shit, Josilin. Now is not the time."

"Now's exactly the right time we need to address this. If you drive off and go home, don't even think about coming back."

"Fine. I won't."

She gasped. "Really?"

I swiped my hand over my face. I was tired of this shit. Having a side bitch took too much out of me. Pops told me this day would come. The day that I'd grow up and start acting like a man. It was time for me to put an end to this relationship.

"You. know how I feel about you," I told her, trying to keep things from escalating. "But I can't do this anymore."

"Don't worry," she replied snidely. "Because I can't either. I just wanted to give you a chance."

I smirked. "A chance to do what?"

"You'll see. I haven't done nothing but right by you. I don't say nothing about this hurtful shit that you do. All I ask for is one night out the week and you can't give me that."

"Josilin, look what's goin' on. You know niggas is out lookin' for me, yet you still made me take you out."

"I made you? Wow. And I'm supposed to believe that you love me?" She opened the door and got out. "Make sure you remember that. Since I made you take me out, I won't make you sit here an other second." She slammed the door.

"She slammed the door and then what?" a detective asked.

"I went home."

The detective chuckled. "Jesus. What did you do when you went home? Either you can be more specific about what happened that night, or I can add your unwillingness to cooperate to the growing list of evidence we've got against you."

"Y'all ain't got shit on me. I told you everything I done that night."

"Did you? From the looks of this report, I don't see anything in here about who killed her."

"Do you think if I knew who killed her, I wouldn't tell you?"

"I don't know, would you?"

I laid my head back on the pillow and covered my face with both hands. "You people kill me. If I was such a bad person like you say I am, who's to say the person that killed Josilin ain't already dead?"

"I advise you to tread lightly, Mr. Dunlap. You are one swipe of my pen away from not being there to bury your father."

"Ain't nothin' gon' stop me from doin' that."

"I can. And if you keep runnin' your mouth, I'll prove it to you." He stood to leave. "Out of respect for your father I'll give you a few more days to soak all of this in."

"That's all my Pops' friendship was worth to you? One day? That's all you can give his only son to mourn?"

"You of all people should know how much your father's friendship meant to me."

"Well, why won't you just leave me the fuck alone? If y'all's friendship meant so—"

"Stop right there! My friendship with your father had nothing to do with you. Just like you don't care that I'm trying to do my job, I don't care who I have to put in prison to make sure my job gets done."

I guess that was his grand closing statement. He walked out of my room with not so much as a glance back in my direction. As much as he disliked me, I knew without a doubt he'd help me if he could. Him and Pops had known each other for years. If anything, he was one of the last few people I could trust.

***

Stutter
15 years ago

The world finally felt like a place worth living in. Every day, I felt stronger, more confident, less pressed to be somebody. Being broke had my thoughts running rampant. I used to wake up and try to figure out what I was going to eat. Now, I was trying to decide if I wanted to recount the 5 G's I had stuffed in a shoebox. I'd counted it more than 1,008 times. I hadn't ever had that kind of money. Kevin hadn't either. In the back of my mind, I kept hearing a soft voice telling me, *Get more!*

Luckily, Sip gave me his number that night at the club. While Kevin and DP soaked up the love from the girls, Sip stepped to me and said, "I want to thank you for what you done the other night. Most new niggas wouldn't have the balls to do what you did."

"B-b-but I ain't m-m-most new niggas," I replied jokingly.

He chuckled. "I can attest to that. You ain't new this shit by far. I could tell by the way you handled the situation. Whoever taught you the game showed you the right way." He handed me his card. "We need brothers like you on our team. Niggas that's built to go when it's time to go. Brothers that already know what to do when it counts. If you're ever in need of anything, don't hesitate to call."

The card was blank outside of a phone number scribbled in the center of it. I tucked the card, although Kevin already had their number.

Weeks would pass since the night at the club. Out of respect for Kevin, I hadn't called Sip. Not that the idea hadn't crossed my mind numerous times a day. I even went so far as to walk to the pay phone and dial the number, only to hang up as soon as it rang.

Click!

Kevin may have been my nigga, but he was moving at a snail's pace. He could still live comfortably if he stopped hustling. Neither one of my parents would stand for that. If one of us hustled, we all hustled. That's the only way I knew how to survive. I told myself I'd give Kevin a little more time to get his head together. Since I've never lost someone close to me, I had no idea what he was going through. But, when a couple more weeks had passed and he hadn't so much as hinted towards making some money, I made the call.

"Is-is-is S-s-sip—"

"I'm here," he replied. "No need for names when you call this number. I know who you are and you know who I am. Understand?"

"B-b-bet."

"I take it if you're calling me, you must be ready. Stop by the shop as soon as you get a chance." The line went dead.

Now what? I couldn't go to Kevin and ask him for a ride. I didn't want him to feel like I was trying to cut him out. I couldn't ask Leonard for a ride because he'd most definitely want in. The only thing I could think to do was rent a car and drive to the shop by myself.

At dark-thirty, I was on the lookout to see what Leonard's next move would be. Dark-thirty was his usual time to get out and about.

I waited on the porch until well after 7 o'clock. When I felt certain he wasn't going anywhere, I put my plan in motion.

The neighbor walked outside, headed to his car. I whistled, trying to catch his attention, but he didn't hear me. He kept walking, so I whistled again. He stopped.

"H-h-how much you charge t-to use your car?"

Our neighbor looked at me skeptically and readjusted his hat. "L told you to come ask me that?"

I shook my head. "No. Th-th-this for me. I'll have it back before mornin' if-if-if you're interested."

He appeared to think about it and scratched his beard. "I ain't neva saw you drive no car. You sure you know what you doin'?"

"I'm sure he does!" Leonard said as he approached. "Go on and give him the keys. I'll settle up with you later."

Our neighbor tossed me the keys without a second thought. Whatever deal him and Leonard had worked out, they'd stuck to it religiously over the years. Usually, our neighbor wouldn't so much as look in my direction. He only did business with Leonard. No one else.

"Where you was on your way to?" Leonard asked. "I can give you a ride if you need a lift."

"N-n-nah. I'm c-c-cool. I j-j-just wanted to take th-the car out for a spin. Brush up-up-up on my driving a little."

He smiled. "Sounds like something I may be able to help you with. Get in."

There was no way I was about to let him fuck this up. I wasn't about to spend the night on dope fiend missions that he'd be the only one to benefit from. If I had to, I was ready to move out. This business with Sip was the best thing that ever happened for me.

"Put the key in the ignition and turn the car on," Leonard said.

I followed every step he said down to the letter, although I already knew

how to drive. Before I knew it, I was pushing 70 down I-35. Leonard sat quietly on the passenger side, bobbing his head to the music. He removed a joint from his pocket and lit it. It was a primo.

"So where were you really on your way to?" Leonard asked.

126

"To-to-to tighten up on m-m-my dri-dri——"

He held up one finger to warn me. If I lied to him, we both knew what would happen to me.

"I was on-on my way to my new job," I admitted reluctantly.

"Which is?"

"At the shop."

He chuckled and hit the crack-laced joint. "You sure that I'm the one you wanna try to fool? I found a nice little stash of cash in the dog house out back. I guess since you've been cleaning cars, ain't no way you could've made that kinda money. Must be some money I forgot I had."

"That's—my—money."

"It's on my property, so it's my money!"

I wasn't about to go through this with him. I wasn't taking no more losses. I hit my blinker to get off the highway.

Leonard grabbed the steering wheel. "The hell you think. you doin'?" he snarled. "Didn't nobody tell you to get off the road. Keep straight."

"That's my money! I-I-I put in the work-work for it. It's mine!"

"Nigga, you better count to 3 and make a collect call to Jesus." He hit his joint and cocked the hammer back on That Bitch. "Today just might be your lucky day."

"I-I-I ain't scared to die n-no m-m-more."

"I don't give a damn what you is. Ya dig? You do what the fuck I tell you when I tell you to do it."

"If you shoot me, we both g-g-gon' die."

"Muthafucka, you think that's what this is about? I don't want to kill you. I want in on whatever y'all doing."

"I w-w-want m-my money."

"Nigga, you can have that money. As long as you let me in so I can take care of my family, your money will be right where you left it. I got a wife and a kid at home. I'm willin' to do whateva' it takes."

"I c-can't mess this up. I've got something I need to do. They're expecting me."

"No, they expecting us! I need to meet the people that can afford to pay you all that money for one job."

"Part of that money is-is-is what we got from O-Dawg."

"Okay, well part of it ain't. I want you to call these new friends of yours and tell 'em you've got someone that needs a job."

I shook my head. "C-c-can't d-do it."

"You do still want that money, don't you?"

I drove in silence. There was an exit up ahead. Leonard must've already known what I was thinking and said, "If you touch that blinker, I'ma shoot you."

"I'd ra-rather d-d-drive off a bridge than let you y-you keep my money."

"I already told your dumb ass you can have the money. I want in so I can get my own money." I spared a peek just to look him in the eyes. He wasn't lying.

"I'm-I'm g-g-going to stop at the gas station to make the call. I-I don't k-k-know what they g-g-gon' say."

"Well, know that if they don't let me in, that five-thousand is mine."

Chapter 16
Stutter

"So, this is the man that needed a job?" DP asked skeptically. He eyed Leonard from head to toe.

"Y-y-yeah. H-h-he's my dad."

Sips eyes lit up. "Oh, so this is who taught you to do what you done the other night?"

I nodded.

"Just 'cause he taught you how to pull a trigger don't mean he built for what we do." DP stated matter-of-factly.

"I've been puttin' in work long before you was born," Leonard replied in his own defense. "Whatever Stutter can do, I can do ten times better."

DP chuckled. "Whateva you say, pops. It's your world. I'm just trying to get a nut."

"The name's L. If you wanna address me, address me by that. I'm not here lookin' for no handouts. I'm here to offer my services for higher." Leonard swiped at his checkered blue flannel as if it was a suit jacket.

DP walked over to Sip and said, "It's on you. If you decide to let him do this, then you gotta be responsible for him. The job calls for no mishaps."

"I can handle it," Leonard said.

They both looked at him. Even though he looked like a smoker, they knew he was the truth. His reputation far preceded him.

"Tonight must be your lucky night," Sip said. "I got a job that'll pay us three grand a piece."

Leonard whistled. "That's a hefty payoff for the first night on the job."

"That's why I said, tonight must be your lucky night."

"Y'all are fo' sho' it's $12,000 layin' somewhere that we're gonna split?"

"No," DP stated sternly. "We have a job that pays $3,000 apiece."

"Why is it $3,000? What are we—"

"Take it, or leave it."

"My man," Leonard replied with a smile. "You can count me in. I didn't come here to complain. I'm just simply trying to understand exactly what we're gettin' off into."

"I knew it was something about you I liked," Sip said. "You're gonna be easy to get along with, because you don't ask too many questions."

Leonard gave me a look that confirmed what I had assumed. DP and Sip were getting over on us.

Sip went on to give us the rundown of the job we were about to do. DP stood against the wall watching Leonard's every move. It was obvious he didn't trust him, probably didn't even like him. But, by the time it was all said and done, I knew they'd love him.

"Where y'all gonna be while all this goes down?" Leonard asked.

"Watching," Sip replied. "I need to know you still built for this."

Leonard chuckled and said, "Well, it don't make sense to keep standin' around doin' all this talkin'. If it's a point I gotta prove, then watch me work."

On this occasion, Leonard was appointed as driver. He drove the Lincoln to the south side while DP and Sip rode in the back. Luckily, they had a regular size wheel in one of the storage units. After we'd switched tires out, we made a stop at a Mexican restaurant on the southside. Sip and DP went inside while Leonard and I waited in the car.

"They fuckin' us real good," Leonard said. "I'm willing to bet whatever we there to get is worth way more than what they tellin' us."

"B-b-but we still getting three G's apiece." I tried to reason with him.

"For now. The price of labor goes up when I have a better understanding on what we doing. Thirty thousand dollars ain't always gon' be layin' in some warehouse for the taking. Sometimes, we might have to put in some work. And when bodies drop, the cost triples!"

DP and Sip walked back out to the car, but they'd brought someone with them.

A Hispanic man strolled around to my window and I lowered it.

"So you must be the one everyone is speaking so highly of." He extended his hand. "My name is Fifty. I'm your inside guy." He paused and peered over at Leonard. Leonard stared back at him mockingly. I guess Fifty didn't like what he saw. "This your dad, huh?" He went on to say.

Leonard cleared his throat. "The name's L. Pleased to meet you." He held out his hand.

They shook.

"Let me know how things work out with this new guy," Fifty said. "This crew might be a little too rough around the edges. Hopefully, this arrangement will work."

When Leonard got back on the highway, we rode in dead silence. All I could hear was the tires roll over the creases in the highway, or an occasional grunt. I thought surely he'd say something about what Fifty had said, but he didn't.

He put on the tape.

"Everybody Loves the Sunshine", Roy Ayers. I'd heard that song more than 1,008 times. Over and over and over again. It was on the tape. Every time we went on a mission, Leonard played the tape. Something was about to happen.

Leonard exited the highway once again, but this time we were on SE 29th. It was late for most businesses in the area to be open, but early enough that people were still out and about. We pulled up at a stop light and waited for it to change. I rested my head against the headrest. Headlights appeared in the side mirror. They kept getting closer and closer; they never slowed down. Closer and closer.

"Sunshine! Folks get brown in the sunshine…"

Leonard positioned himself in his seat, trying to get a better look. He saw it too. The vehicle was coming in too fast.

"Feel what I feel when I feel what I feel when I'm feeling…"

A blue pickup truck shot past just as a four-door white sedan crossed the intersection. The truck T-boned the sedan, sending it rolling. Before anyone had a chance to respond, another car came barreling through the intersection. The driver saw the wrecked truck and tried to dodge it. He overcorrected and went flying off the road into a tree.

BOOM!

"Pull over!" DP shouted. "We need to see if anyone is still alive."

"I ain't pullin' over for nobody!" Leonard fired back. "We ain't come all this way to be a hero. We here to make money. The warehouse is just up ahead."

"He's right," Sip chimed in, agreeing with DP. "What if that was someone you loved, or your family member?"

"But it ain't! Fuck those people. Now it's my turn to ask you niggas. Is y'all built for this?"

"Come on, man," Sip said. "The money is always gon' be there."

Leonard scoffed and reluctantly pulled to the side of the road.

The four-door sedan had come to a stop against a fence. The driver's side was caved in and the driver was unconscious. Flames flickered from under the hood.

"A gas line must've been hit!" Leonard said urgently. "The flames are spreading too quickly." He slapped at the flames on the ground, with his flannel.

DP worked diligently to wake up the driver.

"Wake up!" he yelled as he shook her, but she was knocked out cold. "The only way you're gonna survive is if you wake up."

Smoke began to seep into the car through the vents. Moments later, the dash crackled into a blaze.

"Everybody get back!" Leonard shouted. "I can't keep these flames down much longer."

One by one, the people inside the car began to come alive with screams in agony. The fire covered them in a matter of seconds.

Their cries abruptly ended with a loud boom. The gas tank exploded.

I cowered away. not knowing what to expect. When I opened my eyes, I was looking dead at the other car. It was nose first in the side of a tree. While everyone else stared in shock at the growing blaze, I went to have a closer look.

At one time or another, I'm sure this Lexus coupe was considered to be the cream of the crop. Now, it was nothing more than a bunch of twisted metal. The engine had been pushed in, pinning the driver to his seat. He gargled blood and coughed before he stopped moving.

"H-h-hey, y-you alright?" I knew he probably wasn't. His lower body looked as if it were a part of the car. Judging by his clothes and jewelry, he had a lot of money.

I lifted his arm just to see if he'd move, but he didn't. I nudged him. Still nothing. Carefully, I removed an expensive-looking watch from his arm. Just as I began to tuck it away, he grabbed me.

"Help—me," he said just above a whisper.

I snatched my arm away from him and accidentally fell in the grass. The man stared at me until his eyes finally closed. Luckily, I'd tucked the watch just as DP and Leonard ran up.

"He dead?" Leonard asked.

"I-I-I think s-s-so. He ain't m-m-movin'."

"Well, if this son of a bitch is dead, the muthafucka in the truck is damn sho' dead. Now that y'all done seen what you needed to see can we leave?"

DP looked at him with disgust. "How could you be so cold-hearted?"

"I give a damn what you think. I'm not tryin' to go to jail for having these guns."

Reality registered quickly, because I could see it on their faces. We took off back to the car and got in. Leonard wasted no time trying to finish the mission. But with the warehouse only a few blocks away, the mission was called off. Cops would soon be all over the area.

Chapter 17
LaShura

Today was one of those days I needed to get out and do something. Anxiety had my thoughts all over the place, but being broke had me stuck at the house with nothing to do. I'd heard it said that being bored and alone were the perfect ingredients to add to depression. Lord knows I didn't want that to happen. As bad as I wanted someone to talk to, everyone was gone. Vance had taken Nikki out to dinner and a movie. Kevin called and said he was going out of town with his dad. Funny, in all the years I'd known him he'd never been anywhere - until now.

The thought to call Stanley had crossed my mind, but I didn't want to appear weak or desperate. My last option was to go out for a walk. It'd be getting dark soon and I had too much energy I needed to burn.

It's not uncommon to see lots of people out for a stroll in the area. Highland Ridge Apartments was just one complex amongst many others in the area. Although there were so many other apartment buildings, I never saw too many kids. The majority of the residents were young couples just starting their adult lives. I always enjoyed a peaceful walk and the opportunity to get my thoughts together.

A woman in a brown Audi honked as she drove past. I waved back with a smile. It was little interactions like that that helped to get me through this foreign territory of feeling alone. Most times, all I needed was someone to see me. Someone to acknowledge me. Someone to validate my existence. It's easy to feel invisible when I feel alone. It's like watching the world go by while being trapped in a tiny bubble. Nikki said whenever I feel this way, say the Lord's Prayer as a reminder that I am not alone.

I smiled. Everything was about the Lord with Nikki. In fact, being around her so much got me thinking about the Lord. When was he going to touch my life like he did with her? I suppose, because of my trust issues, I didn't feel his presence. But if I couldn't trust the man I loved, how could I trust a god I couldn't see?

Not long after I went out for a stroll, I encountered a man asking if I had a moment to fill out a questionnaire. He was an older man, tall, brown-skinned with beautiful long white dreadlocks. His beard was just as white as the hair on his head and neatly trimmed. He was so well-mannered and nicely-dressed. I instantly began to inquire as to why he was there.

"Are you from a church?" I asked.

He shook his head. "No. I'm just here to do the Lord's work."

That didn't sound right. "Most people that do the Lord's work, belong to a church."

"I belong to God. He is more than sufficient."

"Oookay. Well, I'm really not too good with bible stuff. I'm just out having a little *me time* before the sun goes down. I'm probably the wrong person to talk to if you're trying to find something out."

"Actually, you're exactly who I need to talk to," the man insisted. "If I can bother you for ten minutes of your time, I'll pay you $100."

Bingo! That was a bottle of Alize and a sack if I could persuade Uncle Tim to hit the highway for a little gas money.

"So, what do I have to do? Fill out some papers and you'll give me $100?"

"How about something better? I just need to ask you a few questions from this pamphlet—" he waved it in the air, "—and I'll pay you for your honesty. How's that sound?"

"Great! What's the first question?"

"Do you believe that it takes communication to have a healthy relationship?"

"Absolutely. You have no idea. That question hits home in so many different areas." I sighed and shook my head.

"How so?" he inquired.

"It's kind of difficult to explain. It has been awhile since my ex and I broke up. Then there's my brother. He was murdered. I feel like in both instances, had there been more communication, the outcome would've been different."

"Interesting," he said and fiddled with a pamphlet he'd been holding. He looked as if he was searching for the right words to say. "My condolences to your loved ones. I didn't mean to open up any old wounds so if you'd please, I'd like to continue on with the survey . What does the word living mean to you?"

"Living means I'm alive. I'm able to do things. Experience things."

"Good or bad?"

I nodded.

"So in a nutshell, living is being alive and being able to experience things?"

"I'd say so, yes."

"And what does the word knowledge mean to you?"

"Knowledge is something that I know. Fact."

"And how is knowledge acquired?"

"Through research, living, and learning."

He smiled. "Sounds like somebody went to college. You are about to ace this thing with no problem."

I laughed. "For this to be a questionnaire, you're not filling out none of my answers in your pamphlet."

His smile faded. "Would you like me to?"

"No, I was just messing around. Go ahead and finish however you'd like so I can get my $100."

He nodded. "Have you ever heard of The Tree of Knowledge of Good and Evil?"

He got me there. I had to think about that one for a moment. I'd heard of a cedar tree, apple tree, oak tree, even a plum tree.

"It's in the bible," the man went on to say. "In the book of Genesis, Adam and Eve ate from The Tree of Knowledge of Good and Evil and because of it, they were banished from the Garden of Eden to work the ground, from which man was taken."

"I remember the story, but vaguely."

"My next question, I'd like you to really give some thought to it before you respond. Understand, this question is not to imply that you should do anything. This question is simply something for you to meditate on, okay?"

I shrugged. "Okay."

"Would you have eaten from The Tree of Knowledge of Good and Evil?"

I didn't have to know much about the bible to answer that. All I had to think about was what happened to my brother, my mother, my father, Uncle Tim, Nikki; the list goes on and on. Just as I began to answer the question, a car playing loud music drove past. I'd had my back to the street when the car passed. When I turned to look, I noticed it was Stanley.

"Take all the time you need," the man said. "I understand how deeply troubling such a question may be."

"No, I was just—" Thinking, thinking, thinking, mad as hell. I watched as Stanley's car turned into Nikki's apartment complex. My mind started racing.

"The man cleared his throat. "Your answer, please."

"No," I blurted out. "I wouldn't eat from The Tree of Knowledge of Good and Evil. Isn't that the reason the world is so screwed up to began with?"

"Possibly. But isn't knowledge acquired through living and learning, which has good and bad outcomes? That's how we learn, is it not?"

I didn't want to be rude, but my patience had run thin. This was the second time I'd seen Stanley's car around Nikki's apartments. I tried to reason that maybe he was there to see me, but that wouldn't be right. That would be disrespecting Nikki.

"One last question and the money is yours," the man said. "If God said you could go to heaven right now, but you couldn't take any of your possessions or loved ones, would you go?"

Honestly, I'd been through enough. I was still trying to heal from all the losses I'd been taking. I loved my family, friends, and this whole experience called life. I could only hope God was as un-derstanding as Nikki said he'd be.

"If God said I could come up to heaven right now, obviously it'd be because of something good I've done. Whatever that good thing I done was, I'd want to teach my family and friends so they could go to heaven."

"After everything you've been through and everything you've seen, that is what you'd choose to do?"

I shrugged. "Why not? Ain't it all about helping people change?"

He smiled and handed me a hundred-dollar bill and said, "Nothing will ever change in this system of things. What is law, is law. If you throw something up

it must come back down. That is the way of this system of things. The Fruit."

Had I not just seen Stanley's car, I would've hit him with a slew of more questions. I was beyond desperate to know what was going on.

***

Leonard
Later that night

I circled around The Ghetto twice. The lookouts seated on the porch steps didn't seem to notice. Someone in a red skully had their undivided attention. Not once did either of the lookouts notice the car I was in. Although the dark tint concealed my identity, everyone knew I drove the Lincoln.

On the street behind The Ghetto was an alternative school. Weeknights there were usually several cars parked out front. The extra cars on the block made it easy for me to blend in and not draw too much attention. I parked behind a white van and got out. An alley ran north and south along the west side of The Ghetto. I crept along the path until I reached the gate just outside the club door. Part of me wanted to go in guns blazing and kill every muthafucka in sight. The other part of me still needed answers, which was why I remained calm as I went inside.

"L!" Nate exclaimed. "What in God's name are you doin' here?"

I put my finger to my lips and closed the door behind me. Nate sat at a nearby table alone.

"Are you the only one here?" I asked.

Nate looked confused. "Yeah. I mean, no. You didn't see those three fellas sittin' outside?"

"I saw 'em, but I came through the side gate so they wouldn't see me."

Nate looked troubled. He got up from the table and waved for me to follow him. He led me across the room through the kitchen and into the back room. The room had a window we used if we needed to make a quick escape. The back door was barricaded just in case the police raided.

"Them boys find out you in here, they gon' try and kill us both. What was so important that you'd risk puttin' us both in jeopardy?"

"I'm here to see your boss."

"Cabbage?"

I nodded.

"You here to see the one person in the whole wide world that you shouldn't be lookin' for."

"The way I see it, him and me got some unfinished business."

Nate scoffed. "Maaan, you sharper than that. You killed that muthafucka's brotha right in front of him. You killed his friends too. Now that I think about it, you killed your lady friend - his lady. I think it's safe to say Cabbage gets the picture. He knows not to fuck with you."

"This ain't about that. This about what they took from me."

He frowned. "What they done took from you? They paid for everythang, straight up."

"They ain't paid for killin' my momma, or big brother Kenny."

"So you blamin' Cabbage?"

"You muthafuckin' right."

"Nigga, is you listenin'? Them bitch-ass city niggas killed my momma!" Nate lifted the window so I could crawl out.

"You can't blame that on them," he said.

"The hell if I can't! I blame them bitch-ass niggas for all of my misery."

Nate pumped his hands for me to quiet down. "You gon' get us killed if they hear you."

"Them ain't no killas Cabbage got watchin' over you. Obviously, they slippin' on their job if I'm in here talking to you. I stopped by tonight to ask for your help."

"L, you gon' mess up everything good I got goin' for me."

"Nigga, the only thing good you got goin' for you is free dope. You still in the same spot you was in when I met you."

"I could say the same for you. So what sense it make to bite the hand that feeds me?"

I pulled out a thousand dollars and handed it to him. "I'm back, nigga. Cabbage may be round here feedin' you that good dope, but I got something that's better than dope. I got cold hard cash. We can run this city, again. All we gotta do is eliminate the competition."

Nate chuckled while rubbing his eyes. His loyalty to me was like no other. Right or wrong, he'd always had my back. For me to be bringing him a thousand dollars, he knew I had something up my sleeve. He was in.

I laid on The Ghetto for weeks, checking out how things moved. In between a flip here and a lick there, I'd managed to live comfortably while my plan unfolded. Cabbage's men were too sloppy and relaxed. I was able to slip through the side gate and eavesdrop on their conversations at will. I'd creep upstairs to an empty apartment, just above where they were posted.

"The streets finally startin' to get back to normal," a man with gold teeth said.

I'd heard Cabbage's men refer to the man with the gold teeth as Gold Mouth. All the lookouts took orders from him.

"I overheard the big man tell Cabbage, if things continue to cool down, we can open the club back up," another lookout said.

"Did he say anything about when we're supposed to get our next shipment?"

Suddenly it was quiet. I figured he must've given them some sort of head nod, because no one said another word. Whatever them boys were moving, they had to be moving plenty of it. To have armed guards outside your place while nothing is going on was a telltale sign of what kind of money you were dealing with. Whatever they was moving, I made it my mission to find out what it was.

Even if I had to lay on these knuckle-heads for a year, I was determined to see this mission through.

One night, a peculiar sequence of events took place. The lights were off at The Ghetto, except for the red porch light in front of the club. I'd slipped through the side gate and hidden out in my usual spot. Only two men worked that night. Gold Mouth was nowhere to be seen. Traffic had picked up on the block. Even Harold had circled the block a few times. when I heard the familiar growl of his engine pull into the parking lot, I rushed back downstairs to listen in on what was going on.

"Didn't you hear me yell stop?" one of Cabbage's men snapped. He'd run up to Harold's truck with his gun drawn. Harold was parked no more than five feet from the doorway, where I was concealed by darkness.

"Where's Cabbage?" Harold calmly asked.

"Nigga, did you hear what the fuck I just—"

He'd overstepped his boundary and leaned too far in the truck. Harold snatched the gun out of his hands and pointed it back at him in an instant.

"Now, the nigga got the gun," Harold spat. "I'm only gon' ask you one more time. Where...is...Cabbage?"

The other lookout ran up to the passenger side and tried to get in, but the door was locked. He beat on the door.

"Open up!"

"Cabbage haven't been here in weeks," Harold's prisoner snarled. "He was supposed to be here tonight, but he never showed."

The other young lookout kept hitting the side of Harold's truck, demanding he let his partner go.

"Tell him if he hits the side my truck one more time, I'm fixin' to break your fucking nose."

He hesitated. The other guy hit the side of the truck again.

Whap!

Harold broke his nose with the butt of his gun. "Next time I'll knock your front teeth out."

"Alright, alright. Don't hit the fuckin' truck!" he yelled to his partner. "Don't hit the fuckin' truck!"

Harold had both them lame-ass niggas right where he wanted them. It took everything in me not to hop out and blast all they asses. These niggas was some bitches. Point blank. Period.

After a brief exchange of orders, Harold shoved the man away from his truck and backed out of the parking lot. Honestly, I was surprised they didn't light his ass up. Seems to me that'd be the right thang to do. Especially in light of what they were paid to do.

For the rest of the night, I hid out in the empty apartment upstairs. I figured if Cabbage was due on the scene anytime soon, I wanted to be there when he arrived.

Adrian Dulan

Chapter 18
Kevin

Trips to see LaShura soon began to take their toll on me. Not only because of the pressure it put on my pockets, but the strain it put on my car as well. Before I knew it, I needed new brakes, oil change, and new tires. Pops said those were signs that my car needed to be serviced. Me being me, I didn't listen, and that's why my radiator went out, which left me stranded on the side of the road. The worst part about not being mobile was I couldn't see LaShura. Just when it felt like our relationship was about to takeoff to the next level, this happened.

In a way, it kind of was good that my car broke down. My money was hella low because I'd been avoiding the block. I didn't wanna sell dope, rob, steal, or kill. Seeing those bodies done something to a nigga. I refused to do anything unless there was no other option. I told LaShura I was going out of town while I got my car fixed. I figured by the time she saw me again, my money would be long as I-35. I'd put my Cutlass on rims and have it lookin' like something special.

I mobbed up to Stutter's door and knocked. "That Girl" by Stevie Wonder played inside. I bobbed my head to the beat and knocked on the door once again. This time the door was snatched open. It was Leonard.

"It's been a month and two Sundays since the last time we saw you," he said. "To what occasion do we owe thanks for your presence?"

I'd be a fool to feed into his sarcasm. He stayed on some bullshit. "Is Stutter here?"

He gave me a distasteful once-over and stepped aside. Surprisingly, the inside of the house looked halfway decent. Shit wasn't scattered all over the place. The room didn't smell like a mouse had died in it. Even Kathy I looked to be in good spirits. She tapped her lighter against the table to the beat.

"W-w-what's up wit' it, Kev?" Stutter said. He strolled in the living room carrying a fresh pair of Nike Shocks. From the looks of it, everything he had on was new. New socks. New T-shirt. New jeans. Even the gun he had tucked in his waistline looked new.

"Damn, my nigga. You ballin' now?"

Stutter chuckled as he sat in the recliner and slid on his shoes. "Nah," he replied. "I-I-I just wanted t-to try something different."

I nodded my approval. "This is a good look for you, bruh. Let's go outside for a sec so I can holla at you."

The singing and tapping of the lighter had merged into soft humming. Although Stutter's moms and pops appeared to be occupied with crack pipes and Stevie Wonder, they were really trying to tune in to what we had going on.

While Stutter ran to grab his hoodie, I stepped outside on the front porch and lit a Black & Mild. *I sure hope this nigga is going to be feeling what I'm about to tell him*, I thought.

"I called DP early this morning," I said. "He said it was cool to stop by the shop. I take that to mean he's got work for us."

Stutter nodded, but never made eye contact. I passed him the Black & Mild. He puffed at it.

"We supposed to g-g-go lay f-fresh flowers on Grandmother's g-g-grave today," Stutter said. "We supposed to be le-le-leavin' any minute."

That was the first time I'd ever heard him talk about family. Sure, everybody is related to somebody. But Stutter was one of those that no one knew who he was related to.

"You know it'll be dark soon. Why y'all wait so late to leave?"

He shrugged. "Leonard wanted to. He felt it was time that I know t-t-the truth."

"About what?"

The front door opened and Leonard walked outside on the porch. His usual dingy attire had been upgraded to something much nicer. Black slacks, black turtleneck sweater, black boots. The only thing that wasn't new were his Coke bottle glasses. "If you need something out the house, you betta go in there and get it. We rollin' out in five minutes," Leonard said.

Before I could compliment him on how well he'd cleaned up I noticed him grit his teeth. I followed his gaze down the street and spotted Cabbage's white Cadillac headed straight towards us. A four-door gray sedan trailed closely behind. Instantly, the mood turned sour when both cars parked in front of the house.

Stutter reached for his strap.

"Not here," Leonard said to him.

"Kevin!" Cabbage shouted through his window. "Come out here to the street so I can rap with you 'bout something."

Both Leonard and Stutter looked at me skeptically as if I had said it. I didn't want nothing else to do with Cabbage. I was in the process of trying something different.

"Whateva business y'all had before is done," Leonard said on my behalf. "I was there the night that you said it. I heard so myself."

Cabbage chuckled and replied, "Ain't nothin' over until I say it is. And even when I say it's over, shit betta start back moving when I say so."

Leonard strolled down the steps and out to the street with Stutter in tow. Reluctantly, I followed, but I was not about to get fucked off by these trigger-happy niggas.

"What kind of man goes to another man's house just to talk shit from the safety of his car?" Leonard snarled.

"I don t know," Cabbage replied as he and six of his men got out. Maybe you can tell me. I'm not the type that's just gon' pull up and talk shit. I'll run up in yo' shit and kill everythang moving." He winked.

Leonard reached for That Bitch, but it wasn't there. Cabbage and his men reached for their straps and drew down on us.

"Wait!" I shouted and stepped in front of Leonard. "If y'all came here to talk to me, here I am. Nobody needs to get hurt if all you wanna do is talk, right?"

Cabbage glared at me and said, "There's a time and place for everything. But when the tools come out, it means it's time to work."

"Do whatever the fuck you think you can do," Leonard growled.
Maybe I will," Cabbage said and raised his heat.

"Cabbage, no!" I insisted.

The familiar sound of my father's truck caused everyone to look. Pops pulled right up to Cabbage's front bumper and got out. A police siren squawked as an officer parked and got out of his car as well. "

Gentlemen!" he spoke in a commanding voice. "Let me see those hands."

Just as quickly as the guns had appeared, they had disappeared. Cabbage was the only one who stood defiantly clutching his gun.

"Ain't no problems here, Officer," Cabbage said sarcastically. "We simply stopped by to invite our friends to a little sit down."

The cop eyed Cabbage still clutching his pistol. He removed his gun from its holster.

"Kevin, get in the truck," my father insisted.

Cabbage looked as if he knew my father from somewhere. "Harold?"

Pops had a look in his eye that I'd never seen him give anyone. "Not here and not now," he said to Cabbage. "This one here is mine."

Leonard seemingly bristled at their interaction. "Hell, this one is too!" he barked and nudged Stutter towards him. "Did you forget you had another one?"

"Negro, I ain't forgot nothin'!" Pops spat. Why don't you step up and be a real man? Own up to your own bullshit."

"Enough!" the officer shouted. "Now, unless y'all wanna take this family feud up in a cell, I suggest y'all clear this place out. Another unit should be arriving any second."

No sooner had the words left his mouth than another police car crested the top of the hill. Whatever leverage Cabbage felt he had against the one police officer quickly faded. He quickly tucked his gun and got back in his car.

Chapter 19
Kevin

"If you dance with the devil, don't be surprised when your behind ends up gettin' burnt," my father snapped.

We'd come straight home after we left Stutter's crib. Pops and his police friend chopped it up outside for a bit, but by the time Dad came in, he was hot.

"Dad, I don't know what you're talking about. Those people just got there right before you did."

He shook his head and sat down. "You got all the sense, don't you? You think I don't know what's going on around here?"

"If you did, you'd know I wasn't doing nothing. I was visiting Stutter when those other people showed up."

"Those other people," he repeated mockingly. "Cabbage and those people with Cabbage are the wrong people to be foolin' 'round with. It ain't no coincidence all them folks start comin' up dead when the likes of them boys come to town."

I sat on the edge of the sofa. "So you thank he's responsible for killing all those people?"

"If not directly, indirectly. That mess they sellin' come at a mean price. Don't nothing good come from foolin' around with drugs. Some of 'em might get you high, but they killing you at the same time."

"Dad, I swear, I'm not doin' nothing. I don't have nothing to do with Cabbage or his people. I was there to see Stutter."

He stared at me in silence for a moment. I guess he thought I'd switch my story, but I wasn't.

"If you tryin' to do what's right, I'll do anything I can to help you," he said. "You believe that don't you?"

I nodded.

"Good, because I mean it. What them boys 'round there doin', you don't want no parts of it. Trust me. I been there. They the type that's here today and gone tomorrow. It might seem like they gettin' ahead, but they ain't. They gon' get left behind. Watch what I tell you. You put good out, good gon' come back to you. It's simple arithmetic. 1+1=2, 2+2=4…simple arithmetic."

I smirked. "You know I haven't been doin' nothing since James was killed. The only person I go and see is LaShura."

He seemed to ponder that for a moment. "I know you haven't done much," he finally said. "And that's why you'll reap the reward."

"What reward?" I looked around the living room with my palms up. "The only thing I got to show for doin' nothing, is nothing. I still live at home with you, my car is broke down, and I'm broke."

Pops dug in his pocket and removed his key ring. He had several old schools, so his key ring was full. His favorite of them all was a '67 Cougar. He'd been restoring it over the past few years. The engine was hog tight and the interior had been redone, but the paint was the only thang lacking.

He handed me the keys to it. "There. Now you got a car to drive."

"Really? "

He nodded his head. "You betta know it. Whatever I gotta do to help you do right, I'm gon' do it." He dug in his back pocket and removed his wallet. He took out $15 and tried to hand it to me. "Here."

"Dad, I can't."

"Take it."

"Dad, come on. I'm good."

"Boy, if you don't take this money!" He dug in his wallet again and fished out three more dollars.

"Daaad."

"Kevin, take this money."

I took it and tucked it in my pocket.

"I don't want you runnin' behind those people for nothin'," he stated sternly. "Do you understand?"

I nodded.

"What's that? I can't hear you."

"Yeees."

"And don't let me catch my car 'round there in front of The Ghetto. I'm telling you Kevin, it is not gonna be pretty."

"You won't."

"I'm serious."

"You won't."

"Alright. I'ma give you the benefit of the doubt. Use $10 of that that I gave you to put in the tank, and the car could stand to use a quart of oil. Whatever is left over, you have it. I don't care. I don't plan on cookin' tonight, so you might save a few of those coins and grab something from McDonalds."

Later that night, I went to DP's shop. Part of me wanted to stop and see LaShura, but I didn't want her to know I was still in town. If she saw me driving my dad's car then she'd ask about my car. Sooner or later, she'd figure out that my shit was broke down and I didn't have the money to fix it. I figured if I got my hustle on for a month straight, once I showed up again, I'd do something special for her.

When I arrived at the shop, everyone was acting weird. Sip kept going back and forth to the front office as if he was expecting someone. DP was up and down, back and forth, sit down and flip the television channel, and jump right back up again.

"What the fuck? Nigga, is you high?"

DP slightly jumped when I'd asked him that question.

"What?" he asked and tried to appear normal.

"Are you high?"

"Nigga, fuck no. I'm trying to listen to see if I hear something outside."

"Is there supposed to be something going on outside?"

"Nah. I saw some muthafuckas snooping around tryin' to peep shit. They look like the feds."

"What was they doin'?"

He shrugged. "I guess watching us."

I leaned in close. "You think it's about those bodies?"

"Nigga, don't—" He gritted his teeth. "Let that shit go, Kev. When it's hot, it's hot. You don't ever know who's listening. You can't make that be the reason why other things are happening. The feds been watchin' us. Ever since my last crew went down, I've been seeing a lotta funny stuff." He straightened his glasses. "You gotta stay game tight and watch out for those haters."

"I didn't know the feds have been snoopin' around already. Yo' shit is hot as a muthafucka!"

"The way I was brought up, a spot ain't a spot unless it's hot. Besides, it might not be the feds anyway. It might've been a city worker snooping around trying to find something."

"But what were they doing?"

He didn't say. Whatever it was, it was enough for him not to hit any more licks. Sip was on the same thing. He claimed to be following DP's lead. As shaky as they'd started acting, I took that as a sign for me to get out of there. When I asked why did he have me come all the way there just to tell me that, he said, "Some things gotta be discussed face to face."

"I understand that, but you could've just chilled and I would've found out later."

"That wasn't the only reason I told you to stop by," he said. "I wanted to tell you about Stutter and L."

"What about them?"

"They're a part of the crew."

"Stutter, yeah, but Leonard?"

"You know it just like I do, he is official."

"But he a dopefiend."

"It don't matter what people think of him. All that matters is he handles his muthafuckin' business."

"I guess it don't matter since you're shutting things down for a while."

"For me, not you. Fifty has some work that needs to be done. He will be here any minute. I just didn't want you to be left in the dark about nothing. If I fucks wit' you, I'm stuck with you."

We shook on that and he went back to the front office.

Not long after Fifty arrived, I knew I could vibe with dude. He was a real mellow cat, laid back, quiet. He dressed casually and didn't wear nothing flashy. He was from Houston, Texas and he had a lot of family scattered around the southside of Oklahoma City. Everything was boom, boom, boom with dude. Quick. Fast. Hurry.

The decision for DP and Sip to lay low couldn't have happened at a worse time. Just when business was starting to look promising, niggas got paranoid and caused business to be at a standstill. To add to his list of growing worries, his girlfriend just had a baby. He'd put a down payment on a new house. Whatever he had to do to stay afloat, he would do it.

"Can I count on you, amigo?" Fifty said.

"Of course, but you still haven't said nothing about what you want me to do."

"For now, pick up and drop off."

"That's it?"

"For now."

I was thinking, why not? I was broke and needed money. I figured I'd be making at least a few thousand. Fifty had a cousin that was a so-called heavyweight in the dope game. He owned a restaurant on the southside, along with two construction companies. Fifty figured since his cousin had so many employees, he wouldn't find out what we were up to.

Fifty made several phone calls to cats I could purchase work from. Once we got past the initial introduction, it was business as usual. All those dudes worked for Pete, Fifty's cousin. That's why we could bank on the powder being A-1 every time. My role was simple. Fifty gave me enough money to purchase four ounces. I would call whoever he told me to call, meet up wherever I was told to, buy the work, and take it to Fifty. Generally, he sold it right on the spot.

"Boom, boom, boom!" he said. "It's not much, but it's something, my friend."

"$200? That's it?"

"I gave you $200 for one day's work. You went and scored for me twice. I paid you $100 for each trip."

"I feel like a sucka. I'm the one taking all the risk while you make all the money."

"You think I make money? I no make money, amigo. This is chicken scratch compared to the money I usually make. I pay $600 per ounce and $300 for the half. I sell the ounce for $800 and the half for $400. How much money did I make if I gave you $100 for the trip?"

"$800."

"Precisely. I take all the risk by trusting you with my money, ideas, dope…" He paused and scratched his head. "Everything."

"What does your ideas got to do with anything?"

"This plan might not necessarily work with you, my friend. These kind of missions means you should have an understanding mindset. You've got to know there's a process at work. Everything will happen in its own time."

"But how am I supposed to survive off this—" I held up the $200, "—until your plan comes together? I spend a chunk of this money on food and gas just to get here."

"I don't know, my friend. There's a lot of people that'll gladly take $200 a day. You can't see the forest because of the tree. I'm creating the perfect image for you."

"How?"

He grabbed me by the shoulders and looked me in the eyes. Those people think you're the one buying the dope, selling the dope and coming back to spend more money. Sooner or later, they're gonna start to trust you. When they do…boom, boom, boom! Take everything."

"For four ounces? Why fuck up a good plug when——"

"We're not, my friend. Trust me. I know these things. I hook you up with four people. When the time is right, you'll hit each one for a quarter key. Boom, boom, boom. Then we split the dope, sell it through my customers, and re-up directly through my cousin."

Pops always said if the numbers don't add up, something ain't right. Robbing his cousin didn't make sense.

"If Pete is such a good connect as you say he is, why rob him? Why not just ask for what we want instead of do something that could get us killed?"

"If Pete finds out I have anything to do with drugs, or anything illegal, he'll kill me. He no want me to do nothing but work, work, work. He make the big bucks. You, me—nada. We make chicken scratch unless we make money by other means."

Now I could see the bigger picture. This dude was a genius with balls the size of cantaloupes. If his plan worked, I'd have a half kilo to myself. I wouldn't ever have to rob, steal, or kill for nothing. From that moment on, I kept my mouth shut and done what I was told. What could've taken me a year to accomplish took form in a matter of weeks.

Stutter was kinda salty about being stuck on the sideline while I got money. Just like I couldn't be mad when he was gettin' money, he shouldn't be mad now that the situation had reversed. Instead of opening myself up to anyone's manipulating guilt trips, I went in grind mode. I'd wake up every morning and link, up with Fifty. Fifty would have me pick up and drop off, then I'd go straight back to the crib. Out of every $200, I at least gave Pops $50 towards fixing my car.

The first time, he wouldn't take the money. He just looked at it. "I'm not taking that," he said and looked at the money as if it were disgusting.

"Come on, Dad. Take it."

"Why I'm gon' take that?"

"To get my car fixed."

His gaze softened. "I don't want nothin' to do with no drug money, Kevin. Don't have me washing your dirty laundry so your hands can stay clean."

"I'm not. I got this money cleaning cars."

He looked at me skeptically.

I showed him DP's card.

"That don't mean nothing." He snapped. "I got 8 or 9 of them things myself."

"It means I got something to show where I made this money."

He couldn't argue with that. Even though he knew I was lying, he couldn't prove it. In a matter of days, I'd paid Pops enough to get my car fixed. I stayed in grind mode because now I could see how Fifty's plan had worked. The people Fifty hooked me up with moved in a pack. No less than two. No more than three. Always where there is lots of traffic. Always.

Daniel, one of Pete's workers, would show up with an older heavy-set Mexican. Dude made no attempt to hide why he was really there. If things ever went sour, he'd be the one after my ass. As the weeks would come and pass, Daniel started showing up alone.

When I told Fifty about it, he said, "It's time."

"What about the other three?"

"Well get them when the time is right. Boom, boom, boom! I get half. You get half."

Chapter 20
Kevin

I slid out of the backseat into an alleyway beside a 7/11 gas station. "Keep your eyes and your ears open," Sip spoke from the passenger window. "Call us when you get somewhere safe."

I slammed the door and DP sped away in the night. I mobbed up the dark alley while adjusting my T-shirt and jeans to cover my strap. When I came out the other side of the alley, instantly I noticed the parking lot was packed. Just the way them muthafuckas like it. Lots of traffic, they could blend in just in case someone was trying to watch them. More traffic was a good thing for me, as well. I'd need to blend in when I took off running with the work.

"Can I get change for $100, but get it all in 1's?" I asked the store clerk.

She smacked on a piece of gum and blew a bubble. It popped. "You can," she replied. "But you'll need to step aside."

"I'm kinda in a hurry. You think I could get it now?"

She stopped chewing and stared at me. She blinked twice.

I stepped aside.

I stood there and watched while four people went before me. I was boiling. I couldn't afford for Daniel to pull up and see what I was doing. It was bad enough I agreed to pull this off in an area I was unfamiliar with. It got even worse if at any point the timing was off.

The cashier counted out $100 in ones in exchange for my hundred-dollar bill.

"Thanks," I said, being sarcastic. "Now, can I get a paper bag?"

"Look, I already done you a favor by giving you change for a hundred. You ain't even bought nothin'." She smacked on her gum and blew another bubble. It popped.

"You gon' make a nigga buy something just to get a little bitty sack?"

She stopped smacking again and just looked at me. She blinked twice.

I snatched a 25¢ pack of DoubleMint off the rack and slammed it on the counter. "There. Happy?"

"I don't like your attitude," she said snidely while she rang it up.

"I don't like yours either."

She snatched off the receipt and handed it to me. "Have a nice day, sir. Thank you and goodbye."

I stuffed the money in the sack and went back outside. Luckily, Daniel hadn't got there yet. I still needed to figure out how

I was gonna get out of there. I walked to the pay phone and acted like I was using it. Traffic was thick up and down the street. Someone honked at the stoplight. The thump of Mexican music blared inside a truck as it pulled in the parking lot. Across the street was a Wall Greens. The parking lot was packed. A police car was parked near the front door. I couldn't tell if someone was in it.

Fuck it.

My best route was through the alley and down the street behind 7/11.

Hopefully I could find some place to hide and call DP.

My cell phone rang. It was Daniel.

"Hello."

"What is happening with you, my friend?" Daniel asked. "Are you at the store or not?"

"I've been here waiting on you for ten minutes. I was startin' to think you weren't going to show."

"Oh, I sorry vato. We'll be there in one minute."

The line went dead.

Fuck! He said "we'll"? Two wasn't the plan. Everything was based on how comfortable Daniel had gotten with me. He didn't even count the money any more. He simply stuffed it in his pocket and we began our transaction ritual. He checked the rearview and the side mirror, then slid the package across the seat.

My turn.

I tucked the work, checked the store, then the side mirror and got out. No hi, bye, nothing. Outro. If someone else was with him, he seemed to pay more attention. Whoever was with him must have outranked him. He always showed them the money.

I hurried back to the alley and called DP. He answered on the first ring.

"You ready?" he asked.

"Yeah. No. I mean, I don't know. Dude say he got someone with him."

"Who?"

I explained how the scenario went down when I talked to Daniel over the phone.

"It's on you," DP said. "Either I can come get you, or you can figure out a way to make it happen."

I thought about it for a moment. I didn't want to fuck this up. It had been almost a month since I had seen or talked to LaShura. I needed this shit to go right more than anything.

My phone line beeped.

"That's Daniel," I told DP.

"So what do you want me to do?"

"I'll call you back."

I switched lines.

"Hello."

"My friend? We here. I no see you nowhere."

I came out of the alley and instantly spotted Daniel's red Honda Accord. There were cars in every parking spot. All the gas pumps were full. People were coming and going. My legs started getting heavy. *Do it*, I told myself.

I strolled over to the passenger window and leaned on the door. "My friend."

Daniel said. "You no get in the car, or not?"

I gave the passenger a quick once-over, like he was the problem. "Nah, not this time. Too many people. Three's a crowd."

"You got the cash?"

"Don't I always?"

He didn't waste another second. He passed a small brick to the passenger. The passenger tried to hand it to me. That was too easy. Then I remembered the cop across the street.

"Whoa, whoa, whoa, one-time is across the street."

The passenger gasped. "Policia! Policia!" He slammed his fist into the dashboard. Daniel put the car in reverse and burned rubber out the parking lot.

People were looking at me as if I'd done something wrong. I strolled to the alley, but not before giving everyone the high-flying middle finger. I pulled and called DP. He answered on the first ring.

"You straight? You ready for me to come get you?" DP asked.

"Hell yeah. I'm standing in the alleyway where you dropped me off at. Man, you wouldn't believe what just happened."

"Quit beatin' around the bush and tell me."

"They left."

"Gone?"

"Outro."

I went on to explain in depth what had happened. While I was talking, DP had started on his way to get me. I was sitting on a ledge that separated 7/11 property from neighboring businesses. I noticed movement out the corner of my eye. A girl that had been giving me a funny look was standing at the entrance of the alleyway. I figured she must've felt some type of way to be staring down an alley at a nigga sitting in the dark. Yet as I went on to tell DP the rest of my story, the girl started towards me.

She stopped when she was in front of me and asked. "Are you the police?"

"*Am I the what*? Fuck no!"

She stared intently at me for a moment and nodded approvingly. "Okay." She went back down the alley.

"Did you hear that shit?" I asked DP.

"Every last word. Sounds like they thought you were sayin' you was the cops."

I laughed, realizing what could have happened. "Figures." I watched as the girl got in a purple Grand Am parked at the entrance of the alley. For the first time, I noticed a dark-colored van beside it. It was loaded down with Mexicans and all of them were looking at me.

Fuck!

"What's wrong?" DP asked.

"They been watching me the whole time." I told him about the car the girl had got in and the van full of Mexicans with their faces literally glued to the windshield.

"Go ahead and leave, bro. I'll meet you on the next street in two minutes."

My phone line beeped. It was Daniel.

"Go on and leave, bro. I'm on my way to get you."

"Fuck that. This is my chance. I'll hit you right back."

Click.

I switched to the other line.

"Hello?"

"I sorry, amigo." Daniel said. "My friend say he thought you policia."

"I ain't say I was the police. I was tryin' to warn y'all about the cop across the street."

He laughed at the foolishness of it all. "I sorry, my friend. You still there?"

"Yeah."

"I'll be there in five minutes."

The phone line went dead.

This time when Daniel pulled up, I knew exactly what to do. When they handed that shit to me this time, I was just going to take it and go. Whoever got in my way would get run over.

Daniel called as soon as he pulled in the parking lot. I emerged from the alley, but he'd yet to park. His car idled in front of the store. I walked over to the passenger side door.

"Get in," Daniel said.

"Oh, uhhh…" He was alone this time. It was totally unexpected. I had to force myself to open the door and get inside.

He pulled away.

"I sorry again, my friend." Daniel said. "I no mean for this to happen—"

"Whoa, whoa, whoa! Where are we going?"

"You still want the coca, no?"

"Yeah, but I thought——"

He chuckled. "Relax, amigo. You with me, now. I take you to my hood and show you how us real vatos do it." He made a right, left, right, left, drove straight down a residential street. He pulled in a driveway and cut the car off. The purple Grand AM parked on the street behind us and the dark-colored van parked behind the Grand AM. No one moved.

"You scared?" Daniel asked.

"The fuck I gotta be scared for?"

"I said that because of the way you're acting, vato. All jumpy and shit. Like you got ants in your pants."

I sat back and tried to appear calm, cool, relaxed. "I'm good." I said. "I just want to get this shit over."

The guy that had been sitting on the passenger side earlier stood in the doorway of the house. He spoke to Daniel in Spanish. Moments later, he strolled out to the car carrying a small brick wrapped in plastic. He handed it to me through the passenger side window. I passed it right over to Daniel.

"What, you no want it?" he said.

"Yeah. I, uhhh——" Thinking, thinking, thinking... "I was just wondering, did you have a scale?"

Daniel spoke to the other ese. He shook his head. "He say, no have no scale."

The man turned and went back in the house.

I removed a paper sack from my pocket and handed it to Daniel.

"This all the money?" Daniel asked as he skeptically looked over the sack.

"Ain't it always?" I picked up the small brick off the seat. For the first time, I noticed Daniel was wearing an earpiece. He was mumbling something in

Spanish. I went with my move and whipped out my burner. "Don't move."

Daniel dropped the sack and said, "I won't, just don't shoot."

I opened the door just as the sliding door on the van came open. I fired a shot in the air.

Boom!

Even silence fell silent that night. First came the harmony of the sound of the city, trucks, cars, sirens. A dog barked in the distance. I bolted down the alley. The residential alley was much darker than the one at 7/11. Dogs barked as they attacked the fences on both sides of the alley. I ran. All I kept telling myself was to find somewhere to hide and call DP. That's all I kept telling myself, over and over and over again. Towards the end of the alley, I saw the back of a building. The building had a lamp on it. I ran towards the light.

In the back of the building was a partial fence. I ran through an opening and hid behind a five-foot pile of center blocks. If it was going down, it was going down right there.

I said a silent prayer. *Please, Jehovah let me make it. I'm sorry I done this. Please.*

Tires squealed as a car sped around a corner. I heard the engine rev up. Tires squealed as the car raced around another corner.

They were looking for me.

Fuck! Fuck, fuck, fuck, fuck, fuck!

God please don't let me die. I promise I'll do right. Just let me make it back home.

I spared a peek over the pile of bricks. Nothing. My only problem was them dogs barking across the alley. They wouldn't stop barking. They kept barking and barking and barking. This was probably as safe as it was going to get.

I pulled out my phone and called DP. He answered on the first ring.

"Where are you?" he asked while on the verge of panic.

"I'm behind a big building. It has a lamp on it and there's a fence." The phone line was quiet. "There's a dog barking across the alley."

"Is there anything else?"

Shit! "It's dark. You'll see me as soon as you turn in the alley."

"You gon' have to tell me more than that, Kev. What about a street name?"

Fuck! I did not want to leave the safety of my hiding spot. But if I planned to survive, I'd better do something.

"I'll call you back."

Click.

My phone rang.

"Hello."

"Kevin?"

"Who is this?" I peered down at the caller ID. The call was Anonymous. I spared another peek over the pile of center blocks.

"LaShura."

I gasped.

"Is everything all right?" she asked.

Thinking, thinking, thinking. "Yeah, um—"

The line went silent.

I looked at the phone. My battery was dead.

Fuck!

I waited awhile and hit the power button. The phone came on.

"Yes!"

My phone rang.

"Hello."

"What are you doing?" LaShura snapped.

"Hiding."

"What?"

"Hiding!"

"Oh, my God. Kevin."

"Quit talkin' so muthafuckin' loud."

"No. Uh-uh. I'm fixin' to go."

"LaShura, wait. I love you."

Click.

I crept along the back of the building until I'd reached the side. I peeked around the corner. I could see a part of 21 parking lot at the front of the building. The lawn and parking lot was lit up by something bright. I didn't wan to go out in the open, but I didn't want to look suspicious either. I tucked the quarter kilo in the small of my back and held my gun dangled at my side. When I walked in front of the building to see where I was at, I realized God had his protective hedge around me the entire time. The light that lit up the lawn and parking lot came from a gigantic cross in front of the building. I'd been hiding behind a church.

Chapter 21
Kevin
The Present

In a dream, the world is much like the real one, only faded. Like trying to remember what you done yesterday. Faded.

I moved, bouncing through eternity in search of light. Light was food. Light was water. Light was everything to a person starving spiritually. It's not uncommon to pass people on their journey in search of light. Most don't know where to look to find the light, and others are content with how far they've come on their journey.

I inched along the trail, always knowing there was something more, something greater. In the valley of darkness, I had to learn how to move based on feeling and instinct. If I felt weeds and brush start to hinder my step, I'd veered too far off the path. I'd carefully backtrack and continue on my journey.

My parents taught me many things while I was a child. One of the most important was how to pray. When my parents were together, we done everything as a family. We ate, slept, prayed as a family. But when my parents separated, ironically, so did their beliefs. I never paid attention when it was time to pray. Either I was too eager to get the prayer over so I could play, or I'd be too sleepy too care what was going on.

"Kevin, wake up!"

My head popped up. I looked around. I was on my knees beside my bed. It was prayer time.

"I'm not asleep," I told my father. "I said, in Jesus' name. Amen."

"Boy, stop lyin'. I'm standin' right here lookin' at you. Now, get up there and take yo' behind to sleep. Since you ain't got enough energy to pray, we'll look into you going to be a little early from now on."

Momma had to go through the same thing. Every night before bedtime, it was always some extras with me. Momma would come in my bedroom and click on the lamp. Most times I'd be playing asleep.

"Get up, it's time to pray," Momma told me.

Little did she know I'd been waiting for this moment all day. Daycare had been a little rough lately. Couple of new cats outta Jersey made playtime a little more physical than what I was used to.

"Get on your knees next to me so we can pray," Momma said.

"Why I gotta get on my knees?"

"So you can talk to God before you go to sleep."

"But where He gon' be at?"

"Boy, hush up and stop playing. You know I don't do no playing around when it comes to God. Where I taught you God lived?"

I pointed to the ceiling.

"Exactly. So, why you sit there and ask me that silly question?"

"'Cause I need to know why I gotta close my eyes."

Momma sighed as if I were getting on her nerves and said, "Because I said so. You do wanna talk to Him, don't you?"

I nodded.

"Then close your eyes and bow your head, like this." She showed me. "Make sure and lock your fingers together then you'll see Him."

I tried it.

Daddy gave me the same spiel. "Close your eyes and bow your head."

Didn't work. Didn't see nothing. I just ain't said nothing, yet. If Momma hadn't swore up and down that this worked, I wouldn't be giving this another try. I closed my eyes and bowed my head like she'd shown me.

"Dear Heavenly—"

"Wait, Momma." I locked my fingers together tightly. Real tight. So tight that my arms was shaking.

Didn't see nothing.

With my eyes still closed, I looked down at the bed, the floor to the ceiling. I didn't see nothing until I looked towards the lamp.

"Kevin, what are you doing?"

"I still don't see him, yet. All I see is a little orange. Some pink, yellow!

Whap!

I saw God that night.

My parents planted a beautiful garden back when I was a child. The garden was filled with delicious fruits and vegetables. The food was nurtured with the best fertilizers. My mother used one brand while my father used another. The food that grew there was more than sufficient. By the time the teachers came in to cultivate the land, they found a garden bearing delicious fruits and vegetables.

"What is this?" the teacher asked.

"A garden. My parents planted it for me when I was a child."

The teacher sampled the fruit and saw it was good. I was already familiar with rotten apples and sour grapes. So when the teacher asked me which of their seeds would I like to plant in my garden, I replied, "None of them."

I moved.

The streets possessed a glow of their own. Right or wrong. Up or down. You are, or you aren't. You live and you learn. What is, was and will forever and ever be.

I moved.

I had to piss bad. Real bad. I rushed in the bathroom and stood over the stool. I wanted to let it go, but my mind wouldn't let me. I shook it. Come on, piss, gotdamn it! After a few more tries, I washed up and reluctantly went back to bed.

Instantly, I recognized something was very wrong with this picture. All the lights and the machines were off. This was a hospital. The electricity never went out. The only light that shone shined through the blinds. Even in the shadowy darkness, I could see someone was in my bed. Cautiously, I inched towards them. Whoever it was had been perfectly tucked in. I inched closer.

It was LaShura.

"Babe." I grabbed her by the shoulders and tried to pull her into my embrace.

I

She was stiff. She wouldn't budge. Her eyes popped open.

"Just let go," she said.

"Huh?"

"If you love me, you would let go."

Eight simple words. Something I would never do. She moved. I moved.

Bouncing through eternity in search of light. Light is wisdom, knowledge, and understanding. I came to a river and kneeled to have a drink.

I saw a man next to a fire. He reminded me of someone I knew. He wore a scarlet-colored T-shirt that was sleeveless. The sleeves looked as if they'd been ripped away. He was much older than me with long fuzzy braids. He'd been on the road for a long time.

"Come and enjoy a delicious meal with me," the man said. "You look like you could stand to use a bite or two."

Boy, was he right. I'd been on the path for as long as I could remember. My stomach was literally touching my back. I was damn near starving. I sat down next to the warmth of the fire. The man speared a piece of meat from a sizzling skillet and set it on a plate. He quickly sliced off a corner of it and handed it to me.

"Try it," he said.

I chewed on it while sucking in air. "Hot!"

He chuckled. "Tell me if you taste them herbs and spices I used. It's an old family recipe."

I took another bite. Delicious. Didn't taste like any meat I'd ever ate.

In the beginning, there was, is and will always be one big mass of consciousness. Forever and ever. Amen.

Consciousness is like the ocean. Its waves leap for the heavens in their wake. When they slumber, they return back to the ocean, only to return much bigger and stronger another day. Man is like a wave in the ocean. When he manifests himself as a wave, he has the ocean inside him. The ocean is all that is, was, and will forever and ever be.

The man removed a lid from a pot of vegetables and scooped some onto a plate.

"Nah, I'm cool on all that. You've been more than generous already."

"But we're just getting started."

"Too much food will weigh me down. I gotta stay moving."

The man covered the food and set aside his utensils. "Always searchin', aren't you? I showed you all of Eternity, yet you hike the trail just to see a glimpse in time."

"I've got a family that's gotta make it through this shit, somehow. The hour is coming. It's dark out here."

"What sense does it make to leave when you know there could be danger? What else is it you need to see to make you content?"

"I need to see the obstacles in the road so I can make a note of where they're at. When my family comes through here, I can help guide them through the darkness."

The man laughed. "My good friend, Kevin. How could you not see this coming? The only obstacle in the road is you. You've already seen all you needed to see. Your lack of belief is why you continue to search.:

Darkness.

Two solid knocks at the door awakened me from my dream. I stretched.

"Kevin," Pastor Johnson said. "It's a little late to be asleep. I thought surely you'd be up by now."

"Did you somehow manage to forget that I was shot?"

He chuckled. "No."

"Well, what else is there to do if you've been laying in a hospital bed for weeks?"

"Think about home."

"I've thought about home every second of the day. I think about home so much that's what puts me to sleep at night." I sighed. "I'm ready to get outta here."

"Don't worry, you're fixin' to." The pastor sat down next to the bed.

I eagerly searched his face for truth.

"Oh, you didn't know?"

"Know what?"

"You'll be coming home soon," LaShura said.

The world stopped. If not but for a minute, the world stopped. There she was, standing in the doorway with tears streaming down her face.

"Babe."

She ran to me.

We embraced.

"I missed you," I said and stole a kiss.

"I missed you too," she replied and moaned.

All those nights I'd fallen asleep furious because I wanted to be with this woman right here. Now that I had her, I wasn't ever letting go.

"Where's December?"

"With my mother," LaShura replied. "I think they went out for pizza and ice cream while we visited."

"Why didn't you bring her to see me?"

"Like this? December wouldn't understand why Daddy got shot, or why Daddy got police coming in and asking him questions. Or why this, or why that."

I stole another kiss. I loved this woman with all of me. Her lips were soft and sweet. "I missed you." I squeezed her. "I just don't think it's a good idea to be messin' around over there."

"No one goes by my mother's house anymore. It's our house that I'm worried about."

"Our house? Our shit is straight."

She shook her head. "No, it's not. Something's not right."

"The fuck you mean, something's not right?"

Pastor Johnson cleared his throat to remind me he was still in the room. "Maybe you should listen to her. All the signs point to the possibility of something being wrong. Which is why I arranged to have this meeting in the first place."

I frowned. I didn't get it.

"The FBI asked if I'd try and talk some sense into you," he went on to say.

"Apparently, with every cop that shows up, you've been uncooperative."

"I told them all I'm gonna say."

"If I were you, I'd reconsider. There are many different branches of the federal government. Amazingly, you're like prime steak to several of those agencies. The higher-ups want the people that's after you. Everyone else wants you behind bars. They're at a stalemate. It's your move."

Fuck! I closed my eyes and took a moment to digest everything coming my way. Shit was fucked up in the worst way. Not only did I need to get out of there ASAP, I'd need more money if I expected to survive.

"They weren't going to allow me to come see you," LaShura said, about to cry.

"How could they have stopped you?"

"By not telling me where you were at. You're not listed as a patient here. I've called everywhere looking for you. It wasn't until two agents showed up at Momma's—"

"That's why I told you it's not a good idea to be going over there. If the police is comin' through there, you know them other niggas will too."

They had my cell phone number. When they stopped by momma's house, that was just a courtesy visit to let me know they were looking for me. When they called, that meant they were ready to talk. I can only imagine if I didn't respond when I did. They probably would've showed up at the house.

"You keep bringin' up the house. Our shit is straight. Don't nobody know about that place."

"Let's not make this about who knows what," Pastor Johnson chimed in. "The bottom line is, she's scared. Obviously, she's seen something that's made her not wanna go back there."

"Whatever she saw shouldn't have bothered her one bit. I got enough heat out there to hold off an army. So, if you don't mind, I'm trying to get my family somewhere safe until I get there. At this level in the game, everything LaShura sees is gonna look strange. Who can honestly say they ever expected to see all this drama coming our way?" I turned my attention back to LaShura. "Take December back to the crib and stay put until I'm released."

"But I don't wanna be there."

"Babe, please."

She sighed heavily. "Okay. I'll do it. Just promise me that when this is over, it's all over. No more drugs. No more guns. No more violence. Just us."

"I promise."

Chapter 22
Kevin
15 years ago

My first quarter kilo, I had to have it all to myself. After everything I went through to get it, it was only right I didn't have to share. I still needed an avenue to make money while DP and Sip were laying low. Luckily, Fifty had to lay low as well. His cousin had been spending more time at the restaurant. Fifty couldn't risk Pete finding out he'd been selling dope.

Good fortune fell right in my lap. I was able to turn an unfortunate situation into the perfect opportunity to make money. I took the work straight back to the block and did my thang.

The powder was so pure I easily turned the nine ounces into twelve. I could've stepped on the powder some more and it still would've been *drop*. I sold Stutter three zips and we got busy.

Traffic was nonexistent at The Ghetto. Although I always saw Cabbage's car, I never saw him. I learned to wiggle through the cracks and only be seen by few.

I even slowed down on chasing after LaShura. I was in 24/7 grind mode. All work, no play.

Leonard had come up with a plan that would get us all paid. All we had to do was open another spot and let him sell all the work. He'd bring us $1200 on each zip. Lock that in.

It didn't take long and the block started jumping. Cabbage's goons must've caught wind that someone had open shop because they started lurking. At least twenty times a day, they'd pass by Stutter's crib. Once we opened up the other spot, Leonard directed all the traffic to it. If Cabbage's goons thought for a second I was about to slow down or stop getting money, they had another thang coming.

Fifty could get us any type of guns we wanted. Simply knowing that bit of information caused me to move differently. I felt more confident and in control.

Stutter and I started pulling strings from a distance. No one suspected us of anything. Dudes may have seen Leonard at the new spot, but no one paid him no mind. He was still known as a smoker. He wore the same faded, checkered flannel, jeans, and church shoes he'd always worn. Even he had runners. Hell would freeze over before someone found out who was behind the dope flooding the streets.

When the time came to re-up, Stutter and I went in half on half a bird. Since Fifty didn't have dealings with the work while Pete was around. I used one of the connects he'd set me up with. The deal went down with no problems. With the exception of a few new faces, nothing struck me as out of the ordinary. I took the work back to the block and continued using the same recipe.

There was no doubt in my mind Pops knew I was doing something I didn't have no business doing. Every extra dime I got, I invested it in my car. Little by little, I tweaked this and changed that. I kept the car behind Pops' house while all the modifications were made. Surprisingly, Pops never said a word. In his eyes, I was finally putting my money to good use. My mother, on the other hand, wouldn't get off my back. Seemed like everything Pops hadn't said, she did.

"How long are you going to keep doing this?" my mother asked.

It was a late Sunday afternoon. The block had just started pumping when she called before I could leave.

"Doin' what, Momma? I'm not doing nothing."

She scoffed. "Kevin, don't try to lie to me. Just 'cause I can't look you in your eyes don't mean I can't tell when you're lying to me."

I sighed heavily, hoping she'd catch my drift. "Why are you and dad always goin' so hard on me?" I inquired.

"Because that's what parents do."

"Parents do a lot of things."

"Like what, Kevin?"

"Parents live together, they eat together, they do everything together. Why do I have to feel like I missed out on having a normal life? Why ain't you and Dd together?"

"I, um, wait. Don't try to spin this around and make this about me."

"I'm not. I'm just asking because I wanna know the truth. When I ask Dad why y'all ain't together, the conversation always veers towards talking about God."

Momma sighed. Just like she could tell when I was lying, I could tell when I'd got to her. "Your father and I had our differences," she said solemnly.

"About what?"

"Life. Your father and I had a lot of trust issues."

"Did you think he was cheating on you?"

"No, he thought I was cheating on him."

"Were you?"

"Boy, I will hang this phone up in your—"

The line fell silent.

"Remember who you're talking to," Momma growled.

"I was just—"

"Remember—who—you are talking to. I'm not gonna tell you again."

"Yes, ma'am. But I would never disrespe—"

"So now I'm a hoe?"

"No, Momma. I was just—"

"That's exactly what you insinuating."

"Nooo, Momma."

"Yes, it is."

"Momma, would you just listen to me?"

"Shut up." The line fell silent once again. "I'm not one of them $20 hoes you've been foolin' around with. I am your mother. Do you understand me?"

"Yes, but—"

"Ain't no but. I am your mother and not your child. You are not gon' sit there and make this seem like I done something wrong. You the one selling drugs, Kevin. You the one. Not me. You. So don't try to make this seem like, like, like I'm your child, when I'm not."

Cold with it.

Pops was quick to switch thangs up just as quick as Momma was. One minute we could be geared toward this, the next it was that.

"Why won't you tell me something? Every time I ask about you and Mom, you shut down on me."

"What is it you wanna know, Kevin? I'm tired of going back and forth with you."

"Why did you and Mom break up?"

Dad studied me quietly for a moment. His arm rested on the arm rest while he tapped his finger on it. "Your mother has got to learn how to deal with the truth," he finally replied.

"About what?"

"Life."

I chuckled softly. "That's the same thang she said."

"Well, it's the truth. In life, you're gonna make thousands of mistakes; some worse than others; some that help others. But no matter what kind of mistake it is, you have to learn how to deal with the consequences. The consequences are how we learn and is what propels us to do the right or wrong thing the next time we're in a similar situation."

"What kind of mistake did she make?"

Pops held up one finger and hurried off to his room. Moments later when he'd returned, he brought his bible with him.

"There's a scripture that comes to mind when I think about the situation we're dealing with."

"With Mom?"

He nodded. "We were also talking about how long you were gonna be sneaking around here selling dope."

"That's not what we were talking about. We were—"

"Don't try to spin me 'cause you will get spun. Let's talk about the harm you doin' to our community because of this poison you've been sellin'."

Cold with it.

If I didn't want to find myself lost in the sauce, I learned to stay away from certain conversations or situations. Every now and then I'd go home early to spend some time with Pops. But those nights were far and in between. I was getting money now. Money was coming in like clockwork. Stutter and I rode around and got faded every day. Shit me and O-Dawg used to do, except we was trying to get on some hoes. Stutter was on some other shit.

"Nigga, I'ma hook you up with this freak named Nancy," I told Stutter.

"I'm-I'm c-c-cool," he replied.

"We been stuck in this house for days, bruh. We need to at least get a telly and treat ourselves to some bad bitches."

He looked at me with his nose turned up. "W-w-what bad b-b-bitches you know?"

I smirked and gave him a once over. "Plenty."

"W-w-well, when w-was the last time you fucked?"

"Yesterday."

"Stop lyin'! Y-y-you fell asleep right there on the sofa. Remember?"

That was our daily ritual. Some days. we'd get in traffic just to see what was going on. When we let Leonard run the spot, that disconnected us from everythang. All we did was cook, bag it, and front it out. When we wanted a look around, we would jump in the Lincoln. A few times we saw Cabbage's goons out in traffic. Luckily, they didn't see us. Judging by how hard they were trying to see behind our tint, I'd say they suspected it was us. When I explained what had happened to Leonard, he suggested they were looking for another reason. It wasn't until the next morning that I'd find out the truth.

"Mornin', sunshine," a man said and clicked on my light.

I opened my eyes to see Cabbage and two of his men in my bedroom. "Didn't I tell you to stop by and see me?"

I cautiously sat up. "I was, but Pops said——" Fuck! I tried to get up.

"Calm the fuck down," Cabbage spat. "I let him leave for work before I came in to see you. Although, I'd hate for him to come home and find a mess."

"So, what, y'all here to kill me?"

"Not today, maybe tomorrow, or the day after. Depends on how you respond to different things. Today, I'm here to talk about you coming back to work for me."

"For five hunnit a week?"

His men laughed.

"I'm cool."

"I didn't say you had a choice. I said, I'd hate for your old man to come back home to a mess."

"You also said that you weren't going to kill me, either."

"But we can beat ya until you an inch from dying. The story won't stop right there though. We'll be back when you get to feeling better. Depends on how you respond to different things. Check it. I don't like you because you've got a problem with listening. You do shit that could sink a battleship. The only reason I'm here is cause you're still here."

I frowned.

"The people we're in business with are into all type of freaky shit: voodoo, witchcraft, devil worship. These muthafuckas talk to spirits and shit. If the spirit tell 'em to do business with you, it's a done deal. If the spirit tell 'em not to, 9 times out of 10 they'll kill ya."

"So you're forcing me to be your crash dummy for five hunnit a week?"

"It'll be more like $2500 a week from now on. I would've used two of my other men, but these people trust few. The fact that y'all are still alive means the spirit ain't tell 'em to kill ya. We're expecting a new shipment any day now. It's imperative I know where we stand."

At $2500 a week, I could dance to Cabbage's cadence. When our money was long enough, I'd have Leonard put an end to this business arrangement permanently.

Chapter 23
Leonard

Certain things make me think back. Back before I started fucking with this shit. Back when I didn't give a fuck about nothing and would do whatever it took to get the money. Back when I wanted to be a gangsta. Back when I didn't know what came with the lifestyle of a gangsta. Back when I couldn't see beyond what I wanted to see. Back when I turned down that road when I should have went straight. Back when I found out that a bitch ain't shit.

My grandfather used to say, "All you gotta do is watch 'em and listen to 'em. They'll tell you who they is."

That stuck with me. In fact, everything he ever told me stuck with me. Even back when I didn't know what a bitch was, Grandpa's words stuck with me. The only women in my life was Momma and Grandma. They were my examples of how to treat a woman and how to handle a bitch.

Men were in and out of Momma's house as if she offered free room and board. Arguments and fights happened on the daily. If not every day, then every other day. Different man. Different situation. Every fight ended on the same high note.

"You ain't shit but a gold-diggin' bitch!" a man shouted.

"No, you the bitch!" Momma fired back.

"And I'll tell you something else I bet you didn't know," the man said as he strolled up in Momma's face. "Your sex ain't that good either."

"Oh, I know you didn't, you pencil dick muthafucker."

"You stink."

"Well, get out."

"Fine. I didn't wanna be here no way."

"Bye."

"Bye to you too, bitch!"

With Grandma, the word bitch dare not come out of our mouths. When I was a little boy, I had to be careful when it came to going over new words Harold had taught me. I could only use them when I was with him, or alone.

One day in particular, she'd stepped out on the porch to talk to someone. This was a fine time to go over a few riffs.

"Shit, damn, damn, damn, damn, bitch!"

"Baby Leonard, come here."

Something wasn't right. Wasn't no one home but me and Momma. She'd stepped out on the front porch to talk to someone, but I never heard her come back in. I peeked my head into the living room from the bedroom. It was Grandma. I loved that woman with every ounce of my being. I ran to her with my arms extended, ready for her warm embrace, but she grabbed me by the wrist, stopping me.

"What was that last word I heard you say when you were back there cussin'?"

I peered down at the floor. Shit. I knew better than to repeat anything Harold had told me to. Regardless of how young I was, I still knew better than to repeat what I'd said.

I put a boulder on the tip of my pipe and melted it. The sizzling made my stomach bubble. I hit it, kept hitting it and hitting it and hitting it.

"Get off the gas," Nate said. "That's way too much heat. You gon' mess around and crack my shit!"

No sooner had the words left his mouth than the pipe cracked.

Certain things made me think back. Back to the good old days. Back when I could do shit like that. Back when I could fuck a nigga's shit up and he wouldn't give a damn because I was that nigga. Back when I threw coke parties like it was a back-to-school jam. Only people in my inner circle was allowed. I had an endless supply of dope. You could smoke, drank, snort, shoot all the coke you could handle. Back when I first started experimenting with this shit. Back when I met a bitch named Kathy.

"Nooo!" Kathy exclaimed. "I told you not to cum yet."

We'd been at it for well over an hour. She was on her third climax. I'd just came for the first time.

"Don't I get a chance to get mines?" I said and rolled off of her. I lay back on the pillow. She rolled over on top of me.

"No," she said. "I need you going hard for at least another hour." She ground her body into mine and kissed me.

"Easssy. Easssy now."

"I'm trying to," She whined. "I wanna fuck." In her frustration, she snatched her pipe from the nightstand and melted a rock on it. She hit it; kept hitting it and hitting it and hitting it.

"Kathy, slow down!"

The pipe cracked.

"Now, it's your turn." She quickly reloaded the stem and handed it to me. She had a way of doing things that made it hard to see past her. I tried to light the pipe, but she wouldn't stop grinding on me.

"Kathy."

She froze.

I melted the rock at the tip of the pipe and hit it. Kathy ground her body into mine. My dick stiffened.

She moaned, "Give a bitch some of this dick."

"I should've caught it. Not about what she wanted, about who she said she was. I was blinded by the heat of the moment, the thrill of the chase; the drugs, the lust. That's what it was. Lust. It wasn't love. Love wouldn't allow me to let us destroy ourselves.

I hit the pipe.

Certain shit made me think back. Back when I first suspected something was going on. Back when disappearances in the middle of the night were justified by a family emergency that ironically was a situation I wouldn't understand.

I never fussed, complained, or questioned her whereabouts. I simply rolled with the punches.

On nights I didn't hear from Kathy, I'd duck off to a country bar on the west side of town called Hard Times. Most of the people that partied there were Caucasian. Occasionally, a few blacks would stagger in. Either they were students from the local Job Corps, or people just like me, looking to have a good time amongst people that don't know who we are.

I knocked the owner of the bar's wife one night on a humbug. I was warming up the car, fixing to leave, when the front door of the bar flew open. A woman with short blond hair staggered outside. She was drunk out of her mind. She took a few steps and fell flat on her face.

I left her there for a minute. Let her think about where she was and if she ever wanted to end up there again. When I saw that she still had yet to budge, I got out to check on her.

"Hey, Miss. Are you all right?"

The woman struggled to get back up. Her blond hair was draped over her face.

"Help," she groaned.

I was at her side in a flash. "Careful now, don't move too fast. You might have seriously hurt yourself." I helped her back to her feet, then swiped away the dirt from her blue jean mini-skirt and blouse.

"Silly me," she slurred. "How could I have been so clumsy"

"Next time, take it easy on the drinks. Is someone on their way to get you? Or did you drive?"

"Who are you to be askin' me all these questions?" she growled and stumbled forward as if she was about to fall again.

I let her. If she kept hitting the concrete, she would do one of two things. Either she was gon' get back up, or she was gon' stay there. One or the other. Didn't make me no difference.

Splack!

She bit the dirt even harder this time. Ain't no way she was getting back up. I looked around to see if anyone else had saw what I'd seen. We were the only ones outside that night.

Her arm twitched. "Help—me," she said.

I was at her side in a flash. "Maybe you should listen this time," I told her. "Don't move too fast, because you may have seriously hurt yourself."

This time when I helped her up, she had blood in her mouth. Reality had surely settled in.

"I need to go hooome," she slurred.

"Jack should be out here in a minute to carry you home. I'm willing to bet he ain't fixin' to let you drive home in this condition." She glared at me. Jack was her husband. Jack was the owner. Jack was still inside with a few friends having a few more drinks with a few more reasons why Jack wouldn't make it home that night. It was the same scenario every time I went to Hard Times. If not with the owners wife, then another couple, or a student from the local Job Corp.

I drove Jack's wife home despite knowing what the right thing to do was. She navigated me down a long dark street that ran alongside the Guthrie Job Corp. The center had a tall wooden fence down the side and along the back. The fence was mostly covered by trees. The side of the center was where students snuck off to meet people. Simply driving down the road you'd see cars parked to the side. Ain't no question as to what was going on. The only question was who you'd see.

On this particular night, I saw Harold's car parked on the side of the road. I'd heard he was supposed to be getting married. I sure as hell didn't expect to see his car parked along the side of the road. I slowed down as I neared his ride to see inside. Harold's head rested on the head rest. He looked to be sleep.

I kept going.

When I arrived at Christy's house, I had to walk her in because she was too drunk to stand on her own two feet. Once inside, I led her over to the couch so she could get comfortable.

"Thank you," she said while releasing a sigh of relief.

"If you'd like to thank me, do it by giving me a few rounds on the house the next time I come in. Be sure and tell Jack that he owes me big time." I turned to leave.

"Don t go," she said.

I peered back at her, slightly confused, and said, "Excuse me?"

"Stay awhile."

"For what?"

"Come sit next to me and I'll show you."

I sat down next to her, actually thinking she was about to show me something. In a way she did - just not the way I expected.

Christy slid over and reached for my crotch.

"Whoa, there you go moving fast again." I held her at bay by the shoulders. "If Jack come in here and see the mess you tryin' to make, there's gon' be one big misunderstanding."

"Fuck Jack."

"That's your job."

"I'll never sleep with that sorry two-timing son of a bitch again!"

"So this is more like some revenge fucking you trying to do?"

She nodded and lit a cigarette. "Why not? If he gets to run around town fuckin' every bitch that'll let him, I should be able to too."

Ironically, we were in the same boat. Although I didn't know for sure if Kathy was out with another man, I'd be willing to bet my last dollar she was. For the meantime, I decided to keep what I suspected under my hat. Our relationship was fairly new at the time. She was entitled to her mistakes, just like I was entitled to mine.

Needless to say, I slept with Christy that night. I would've never imagined she'd be able to take dick the way she did. Christy was a tall, slender woman. The ruffles in her blouse hid her C-cups perfectly. When she got undressed, everything looked just right in all the right places. I had her lay back so I could hit it missionary on the sofa. She was twenty years my senior. She wanted only what a young stallion could do. Every time her eyes rolled to the back of her head, I instructed her to look at me.

She moaned. "Uhhh!"

There goes that look. That uh oh, I'm in trouble, look. She knew she'd bit off more than she could chew. She showed me her fangs. I showed her mine.

"Take it."

She squirmed around, fighting to do as she'd been told.

The more I kept going, the more her pussy got wet. The more her pussy got wet, the more it began to talk. The more it began to talk, the more she began to fade out.

I gently guided her face back toward mine. "Look at me. If you're not looking me in the eye, then watch what this dick do to you."

I pounded on her pussy.

"Uhhh!" she cried out.

If Jack would've walked in, surely he'd have been jealous. Obviously, she hadn't been getting fucked the way I was fucking her. Off of one fifteen-minute quickie on the sofa, Christy had opened up their home, bank account, and her heart to me. On nights, Kathy would slip away leaving me clueless as to where she'd gone, I'd unwind at Hard Times.

Surprisingly, I'd see Harold's car parked along the road by the center a lot. The damnedest thing about it— he'd always be asleep. I pulled up on him on my way from dropping Christy off and hit my horn.

"The hell is wrong with you, man?" Harold snapped.

"Nigga, you betta watch how the fuck you talk to me."

Surprise registered across his face. "L, that you?"

"Who else you know in a red '57 Chevy?"

He laughed, trying to lighten the mood. "My bad. I thought you were someone else. Besides, what brings you out this way, this time of night?"

"I should be askin' you the same question. I've passed through here on several occasions and saw you out here asleep."

"Asleep? Negro, I wasn't asleep. I was—"

Errr! Errr! Errr!

I spun around in my seat. What the hell was that sound? I grabbed my heat from under the seat, cocked it.

"L, what in the world is you trippin' off of, man?"

I checked the side mirror, the rear-view mirror and down the street. Whatever made that sound was close.

"Messin' around out here by all these trees, ya ass been done got ate up by some wild animal."

Harold looked confused and lay his head back on the headrest. I could tell he was unconcerned about what I'd tried to warn him of.

Errr! Errr! Errr!

I left his ass right there to deal with the consequences. Momma always told me, a hard head makes a soft butt. Didn't make no difference to me what happened to him. He was the one that was gon' have to deal with it.

Not long after I started sleeping with Christy, Jack got his mind right. I don't know if his neighbors told him about the black guy that came over every night when he left for work. Either someone told him or the pussy did. I noticed the smirks when he thought I wasn't looking. So to avoid there being a big misunderstanding that would surely lead to his doom, I called it a night.

I was warming up my car about to leave when the front door to the club flew open. A woman wearing a cream-colored sweater, navy blue skirt, and loafers staggered outside. Her ebony skin and style of dress was a sign she was likely from the Guthrie Job Corps. She took a few steps and fell flat on her face.

Same scenario, different chick. Turns out the young woman was a student at Job Corps, like I'd suspected. She was from Miami, Florida and had been at the center for over six months. She instructed me to park just outside the fence around Job Corp, like everyone else. Ironically, it was in the same spot Harold had parked, before. I was a little leery at first, but decided to go along with her directions.

"I've heard of you," the young woman said. "I heard you were the wrong person to mess with."

I chuckled and shut off my car. I cracked the windows and took a minute to make sure my surroundings were straight. One car was parked further up the road and two more were behind us. Nothing looked suspicious, and I'd yet to hear anything strange. It was a typical quiet but foggy night.

"I don't know if I should take that as a good thing, or a bad thing," I finally replied.

"It depends on what your definition of a good thing is." She gave me a lustful once-over and licked her lips.

Damn. I knew what that meant. It may have been a different chick, but it was always the same scenario when you took someone home from Hard Times. We both understood what people do who parked on this street. Either you were in, or you were out. Either you were fucking, or you weren't.

"What do you say we climb in the back seat so you can stretch out?"

"I've got something better," she said and came within inches of kissing me.

"My ex-boyfriend said I have the best head in the world. Would you like to try some?" She massaged my crotch.

"I see someone likes to go straight in for the kill. You don't do no bullshittin' around, do you?"

She unzipped my pants and pulled my underwear down. I guess she didn't give a damn whether I wanted her to or not. She wanted to suck some dick, so I let her.

Headlights appeared up ahead. I positioned myself in the seat so she could work. Whoever this girl was, she was the truth. Slowly but surely, she worked to deepthroat my dick. I didn't think she could do it. I didn't think she would do it. She kept kissing it and licking it then occasionally sucked the head.

Bullshittin'.

Headlights appeared in the rearview mirror. I closed my eyes and tried to guide her mouth further down my shaft. Each time she came up, she went a little further down. She was going above and beyond any expectations I had. Truthfully, I thought she'd be a waste of my time.

Moments later, I heard the growl of a muscle car as it slowed to a stop next to my car. The horn honked.

"L, you all right over there?"

"What do it look like?" I snapped and glared over at the driver. It was Harold.

"Calm down, lil bro," he said. "I just stop by to check on you. I passed by earlier and you looked like you were asleep. I figured something was up with that, cause that ain't like you."

Errr. Errr. Errr!

I almost fainted. She'd done it. She took all of it. Even Kathy hadn't dared to let my dick slide down her throat. Suddenly, I realized Harold might've been watching. I casually looked over as if I weren't up to something. Harold's eyes were glued to his rearview mirror as if he'd seen something.

"Harold!"

He jumped.

"What in the hell are you doing?"

"I thought I saw—" He paused and peered through the side mirror, checked the rearview mirror again. Nothing.

"Man, ta hell with all that. Are you gonna sit there and look like a damn fool, or say what you've gotta say and get moving?"

Harold gave me that look again; that I wish you were dead look; that I hate you and one day I'll get you back look. But why?

Certain things made me think back.

"L, how long is we gon' keep doing this?" Nate asked. "It's the same shit no matter if you get in the game ten years ago, or now. Either you're gonna make a lotta cash or you're not. Either you're gonna keep it gangsta, or turn snitch. Either you're gonna survive in these streets, or be killed. It's the same shit, now, then and forever and ever."

"Don't start with all that whining and carryin' on 'cause things didn't work out for you like they have for me."

Nate looked at me and scoffed. "Pleeease. Everything is workin' out just fine. It's just sometimes I wanna try something different."

"Like what?"

"I don't know. Something. You don't think I wanna know what it feels like to have kids?"

"Nigga, you too old to be thinking like that."

"I didn't say I wasn't, but you don't think I wanna know?"

"What about me? You don't think I want that?"

"You already got it. You've got a wife at home and a son that's grown."

"That nigga ain't my son."

Nate sighed and shook his head. "He been yours all this time. You raised that boy to be a reflection of you."

"The circumstances of where he grew up made that boy act like me. Besides, he been running behind Kevin since they was in high school."

"That's another one that's been molded into a gangsta by you."

"Neither one of them niggas are a gangsta. If you ask me, both them niggas act like they daddy."

"The apple don't fall too far from the tree. If you pay attention closely, you'll be able to see yourself in the mirror."

Chapter 24
Kevin

Shortly after I arrived on the southside, flashing lights lit up my rearview mirror. I shuddered at the idea of it being the cops and pulled into a liquor store parking lot. A blue Pontiac with tinted windows parked behind me. The driver got out.

"Is the car for sale?" a Hispanic man asked. He was young, overweight with glasses. He spoke with someone in a hushed tone over his cell phone.

"Just hit the number on the sign." I pointed to the For Sale sign in the back window.

"Hold on, hold on, hold on. Let me get a pen and a piece of paper so I can jot this down." He fumbled with his pants pocket, his jacket. "Gimme a break would ya!" he yelled in his phone. "I'm doing ten different things at once." He nervously looked at me and smiled. "My friend is on his way here. He say he wanna see your car."

"Tell your friend I said I'm sorry, but I can't stick around and wait for him to get here. I've got someone that I've gotta meet."

"But, wait! He say he give you whatever you want for the car." He inched closer and said, "Green, white…cash."

He caught me off guard when he said all that. Most people wouldn't feel comfortable letting someone know they had all of that. Dude must've recognized the look of uncertainty on my face because he quickly confirmed what he'd said. "That's right, big dawg. I can get you anything you want. My friend lives just around the corner and he should be here any minute."

I checked my watch. I was late, and there was no guarantee his friend would even buy the car. My eyes drifted down the street. Cars were moving at a snail's pace up and down the block. It was a cloudy day that day, with a light drizzle. The last couple of days had been picture perfect.

Leave.

One word. One opportunity. No time to think about where it came from, or why it suddenly popped in my head. Without another word I went to get back in my car.

"Wait!"

Something didn't feel right. I reached under the seat and grabbed my strap. Dude ran up to my door and tried to open it. Locked.

Bam! Bam! Bam! He beat on my window. "Open up!"

I raised my heat. He froze. Should I shoot this muthafucka?

Drive.

What should I do?

Drive!

I sped out of the parking lot. After I'd hit a few corners and finally calmed down, I pulled into a Sonic and parked in the back. My mind raced to figure out what had just happened. Was I about to get robbed? Was that some of Daniel's friends out to get revenge?

My phone rang.

It was Phillipe.

"Where are you?" he asked.

My heart was still racing, but I didn't want to alarm the plug. "I'm less than ten away. Is everythang cool? Do you still want me slide through?"

"Hold on, hold on, hold on. Less than ten minutes away? How much you say you want again?"

Now he had me thinking. Was it a sign to go back to Guthrie? "I need half a brick. You still want me to come to the usual place, or not?"

"Hold on, hold on, hold on."

The line was silent. I thought surely he'd disconnected the call, until I heard whispering.

"Hello?"

"Oh, I still here, my friend," he said, chuckling forcefully. "I thought you say you want something else. I no know you want that much. Let me make a few calls."

"But I'm already here."

The line went dead.

Shit. I was hot. I'd drove all this way just to almost get smoked, just to turn around and be forced to stick around to see how long I could stay alive.

Luckily, there was small restaurant close by I'd been meaning to try. The parking lot started on the side of the building and wrapped around to the back. Instead of going through the drive-thru I went inside to eat.

"Hello, is anyone here?" Chairs were stacked neatly on top of the tables, except for one. Mexican music played softly over the loudspeaker.

Moments later, an older woman emerged from the back. She wore a scarlet apron with a name tag with no name on it and glasses too big for her small face.

"May I help you?" she asked.

"Let me get three Ru's Soul Tacos with a large Grape Supreme Soda."

She punched in my order. "Would you like to upgrade your meal with two of our famous house special sauces?"

Fuck it. I liked different thangs, anyway. I quickly paid for my meal and went to sit at the only table that didn't have chairs on it. Not long after, an old black guy brought me my meal.

"You expecting anyone?" he asked and slid my tray in front of me.

"Nah, just killing a little time while I wait on a call. You can take a load off your feet if you'd like."

The man sat down across from me and set his baseball cap on the table. He, too, wore a scarlet apron with a name tag with no name on it.

"We hardly see young fellas like you comin' through the door these days."

"Like me?"

"Young, black, and with so much potential. I'd say if you've ended up here, either you've made a wrong turn or chose the wrong road."

I unwrapped the scarlet paper off of one of the tacos. Chopped fried chicken breast, lettuce, tomatoes, cheese, and sour cream. I dipped the taco in their house special Straight from Hell sauce and tasted it.

"Something to die for, isn't it?" the man asked.

It might have been hot as hell, but it was the best taco I'd ever ate. "I haven't ever had something so hot, but good in my life."

"Lotta folks love it."

"You mean a lot of folks that don't got no taste buds."

The man laughed. "Our sauce is coined Straight from Hell for a reason. Maybe if I changed the name to only good for folks that don't got taste buds, business would pick up."

"All I know is it sure is hot as hell." I took another bite, but could hardly taste anything. A cool burst of sour cream coated my tongue.

"You know, you remind me a lot of me when I was your age," the man said. "Always rippin' and runnin', endin' up some place I ain't got no business being."

I looked at him sideways. "How you know I be rippin' and runnin'? This is the first time I ever ate at this restaurant."

"For starters, I know you ain't from around here. That's the first indicator that you be on the move. Secondly, not many people drive a 1967 Cougar. At least not in these parts. Cars like that…" He paused and scratched his head. "Could be worth a lot of money if you fix 'em up right. You couldn't imagine how many people are out looking for that exact make and model. as we speak. I'd say they're looking for the same color as yours, but I wouldn't want to mislead you."

I finished off the rest of my fried chicken taco while Old School rambled on and on about nothing. For the most part, dude sounded just like Pops; always trying to give a nigga some game but don't even know the half. I blocked him out and kept eating just like I'd do my father.

My concern was Phillipe. Whenever we done business in the past, it was in a timely fashion. Never hold on, wait.

I removed the next wrapper, expecting to see another fried chicken taco. To my surprise, popcorn shrimp and fried clams peeked from the side of the taco shell.

"Try the Heavenly Sweet sauce on this one," the man said. "You'll love it."

I dunked my taco in the sauce. Deliciously sweet. Almost too sweet. Damn.

"If I were you, I'd do something with that car," the man said while gazing outside at the traffic. "I wouldn't care if you hide it, sell it, or paint it. Do something with it. A car ain't worth all the trouble you risk getting into just for havin' it."

In the back of my mind I was thinking, had Daniel put the word out on me? That would explain why that car pulled me over when I got to the southside. But, then again, Daniel was a junky. If Pete was half the boss Fifty said he was, he'd have fucked Daniel up and I'd never see him again.

It didn't take long for me to finish off the second taco. I was so anxious to see what the last one was I'd unwrapped it before I'd finished chewing.

"An ordinary taco?" I asked in utter disbelief.

"You did come here to buy a taco, didn't you?"

"Yeah, but you gave me all that exclusive stuff first and then switched it up on me."

The man chuckled. "Life is the same way. First, it's all peaches and cream, then reality sets in."

"What?"

"You did come here to buy a taco, didn't you?"

I went on and finished off the last taco despite how terribly plain it was.

When I tried to place two more orders to take with me, the man said, "Ru's Soul Tacos is closed."

I checked the time. It was a quarter till 7. "Why y'all closing so early?"

"Because it's getting dark out. Too much goes on 'round here when the sun goes down. He gazed out the window at a white Expedition as it pulled in on the side and waited at the back exit.

"Looks like someone else is trying to get some of these Ru's Soul Tacos. Either that, or collect the bounty for finding the needle in the haystack."

The Expedition sped away.

When I went back outside, I noticed the Expedition had returned. This time when it pulled in, it slowed down next to me as I headed to the car. I played it cool like I hadn't peeped their move, but when I got behind the restaurant, I upped my heat on them.

Skerrrr!

The Expedition sped off into the night. Suddenly, my legs felt like jelly. Was everybody on the southside out to get me? While my mind started racing to piece together a reasonable explanation, my cell phone rang.

"Where are you?" Phillipe asked.

"Close," I replied.

"Do you still want it, or no?"

"Of course I do. I've been down here waiting all this time for you."

He chuckled. "I had something I needed to take care of. Come to the apartments and I'll have everything waiting."

That's how business was always done. Call, pick up, and go. In that order.

I was at our usual meeting place in less than ten minutes. Normally, I wouldn't dare have the strap out so Phillipe could see it. Considering all the strange things that had happened, I didn't give a damn who saw it. Once I'd got what I came to get, I headed back to the spot. Stutter and Leonard had been on edge the entire time I'd been gone. They'd even devised a plan to find me if I hadn't returned within the hour.

As the days continued to come and go, my stash got bigger. I started getting antsy to floss a bit. We'd been all work and no play for months. In my eyes, it was only right if we took a little time to enjoy ourselves.

"What do you say we go to the club again?" I asked Stutter.

He shifted uneasily in his seat as if he was giving it some thought. We'd been bored in the house all day.

"We-we n-n-need to be close just in in case we get a call to pick up t-t-the bag."

"Nigga, ain't nobody fixin' to be calling for us to pick nothin' up at 11 o'clock at night. I say we hit up DP and have him get the limo. Then, me and you could hit the mall and buy some new outfits. Fuck it. We may as well call Fifty and let him in on the action. It's been a minute since I've heard from him."

Stutter thought about it, but it didn't take long for him to come up with an answer. Our first night out at the club was a very memorable moment for us. This time, we'd be a little more familiar with what to expect.

Later that evening, I called DP and asked him to reserve the limo for us. Although he wouldn't be tagging along on this particular night, I managed to get Fifty to hang out with us.

"Pull up and park in the front just like you did last time," I informed the driver.

He slowed as he neared the entrance. Cars were bumper to bumper grid-locked. Two officers worked feverishly to untangle the source of the problem.

A small Toyota had overheated up ahead. Antifreeze leaked onto the street.

A woman screamed to get our attention from the sunroof of a Chrysler. Club security stopped us when we pulled in the parking lot.

"You can't park here," the security guard said.

"How come?" I asked from the privacy window. "The only other place to park is at the back of the lot. Then we'll have to walk all the way back here just to get in the club."

"Sounds like you already know what to do. The last time I let this thing in, I got fined for not charging a VIP parking fee."

"How much was the fine?"

"$100. I had to have the guys take extra measures to ensure the safety of everyone."

I peeled off $250 and held it out to him. "This should cover everything you lost and then some. There's another hundred in there if you'll let us park here tonight."

The guard looked at the money as if he couldn't believe his eyes. He quickly stuffed the cash in his pocket and sent another man to set up a perimeter.

Instead of going inside, we chilled outside until the club livened up a bit. Lexus wasn't as packed as before. The people that did go inside didn't do so without gawking at the stretch limousine first.

"This shit is crrrazy, right?" Fifty said while watching the parking lot swell with people coming out to kick it. "All these people. This big-ass limo. These girls."

"Too bad you're a father now with a family at home," I reminded him. "No new pussy for you tonight. All you can do is get drunk and blown away."

He laughed. "I wouldn't have it no other way. I love my girl. I love our baby. I love everything about my new life except my money situation."

I looked in disbelief. "Come on, brah. You're the one settin' up all the licks. What's the hold up? You should already have everythang you need."

"Nah, nah, nah, it don't work like that. It ain't always boom, boom, boom. Sometimes it's slow down. Let's think this thing through for a bit. This thing with DP is starting to have me worried. This ain't like him. It's one thing to get scared and disappear for a day or two. It's an entirely different thing when you get scared and disappear forever!"

"Maybe he saw something that really fucked with his head."

"Or, maybe he knows a little bit more about what's going on than he's telling us. In this game, you trust no one and question everything."

The stuff Fifty had said was as real as it gets, but I wasn't going to be too quick to doubt what DP was doing. I figured, if he was being followed, then he was doing the best thing he could do by not coming around.

"Whatever is going on, I just hope it don't affect us. The last thang we need is more problems just when thangs done finally started looking up."

"For who?" Fifty inquired, mockingly. "Because I know it's not me. I'm slowly fading away, amigo. Who's going to help me in my time of need? I help everyone, but when I need help, no one is around."

"I'll help you, if it comes down to it. Although I'm pretty sure you're just testing me to hear my response."

"Nah, it ain't like that. I wouldn't do that to my new friends, we're like family now. Hospital bills and the cost of living are eating me alive. If DP and Sip won't do it, I need you and your friends to come together so we can do another job."

Hitting another lick was the furthest thing from my mind. If it weren't for the fact that Fifty had looked out for me, this wouldn't be up for discussion. Besides, now that we'd stepped up and bought a half a kilo from Phillipe, it wouldn't be nothing to ask for another one. We could easily kill two birds with one stone, then turn around and re-up with Pete.

By 12 o'clock, we'd made our way in the club and got a table in the back. Of course, Fifty wanted to talk about business, business, business. Everything was about business for the time being. Security practically roped off our area to stop people from coming back to see who we were. Every now and then we'd go back out to the limo and smoke. That was my way of letting people know we were the ones doing it big that night.

As the club hours slowly drifted to a close, the party trickled through the front doors and outside into the parking lot. Traffic was just like it'd been when we arrived. While Stutter and I hung out the windows flirting with all the girls, Fifty took an important phone call from his cousin, Pete.

"He say, he want us to come by the restaurant," Fifty said when he'd disconnected the call.

"R-r-right now?" Stutter asked in disbelief.

Fifty nodded. "That's what he said, amigo. He say you don't have to worry about no food, drinks— nothing. He got everything, just come to the restaurant."

I peered over at Stutter. This was it. This was what we'd been waiting for.

Once we had our own major plug, nothing or no one could stand in our way. If we were lucky, Pete would see the edge he had in dealing with us. Not only could we sew up Guthrie, but we could supply Cabbage and possibly his people.

When we arrived at the restaurant, I couldn't help but notice the long line of Mexicans standing outside. Some of them looked to be as old as my pops. At the far corner of the parking lot sat a green pickup truck with a camper on the back of it. Two Mexicans in skullies and wife beaters mugged us as the driver parked.

"That's Pete, over there," Fifty said while pointing towards Phillipe and a group of men.

Nothing about this dude screamed plug. He looked like an ordinary guy in a white T-shirt, shorts, and white tennis shoes. Nothing flashy. I guess that's where Fifty got his style from. He got out and went to talk to his cousin.

"I wonder what they're over there talking about?" I asked Stutter.

He peered out the window and shrugged. "I-1 don't know. Could be about us, the limo, girls. W-w-whatever it is, they don't look too happy."

Strangely, he was right. Five people surrounded Fifty in a tight circle. His cousin appeared to be fussing at him, but I really couldn't tell. Most of the people around Fifty were taller than he was.

Moments later, Phillipe waved for me to get out. I did, but not before grabbing the bottle of Hennessy and a glass from the bar.

"Look at you. You ballin' now?" Phillipe said as he approached with a mischievous smirk on his face.

"Nah, we just rewarding ourselves for all the hard work we've been puttin' in."

He laughed forcefully and said, "I wish I could be like you. You put in hard work and you get all the money, the girls, cars— everything. When I put in hard work, someone always takes it from me."

Suddenly, I got a nagging feeling that something wasn't right.

Before I could react to it, Phillipe asked, "What's this you are drinking?"

I poured him a glass and handed it to him. He downed it in one gulp. "It's okay, but Mexicans like tequila. We want something strong that'll put you on your back."

I looked over just in time to see Fifty get punched in the stomach. Course, I acted like I hadn't seen shit. When I looked back at Phillipe his mischievous smirk had broadened.

"One minute you buying small, riding around in your old school like you're barely getting by. Now you're riding clean, buying 18 ounces at a time. If I didn't know any better I'd think something was up with that."

"Ain't much to think." I told him. "Me and my nigga, go in half on everythang. I was taught if you hunt as a pack, you have to move as one. We tryin' to get our weight up so we can expand a little."

Phillipe scoffed and spit on the ground. "What do you know about weight? You think cause you buy 4 ounces here and a quarter key there, you're ready to move weight?" He grabbed me by the ear and tried to pull me close to him.

I snatched my head away from him and snarled, "Nigga, you know we don't get down like that." He glared at me for a moment before he spoke to three men standing at the front of the limousine. Each of them wore cowboy hats and boots with their shirts halfway unbuttoned.

I took a swig from the bottle just as I heard a truck pull up behind me. I spared a peek over my shoulder and noticed it was the green truck with the camper on the back of it. 2 ese's got out carrying semi-automatics. I knew when I saw them order Stutter to get out of the limo, we'd made a grave mistake.

To Be Continued...
Forever Gangsta 3
Coming Soon

Adrian Dulan

Lock Down Publications and Ca$h Presents assisted publishing packages.

BASIC PACKAGE $499

Editing

Cover Design

Formatting

UPGRADED PACKAGE $800

Typing

Editing

Cover Design

Formatting

ADVANCE PACKAGE $1,200

Typing

Editing

Cover Design

Formatting

Copyright registration

Proofreading

Upload book to Amazon

LDP SUPREME PACKAGE $1,500

Typing

Editing

Cover Design

Formatting

Copyright registration

Proofreading

Set up Amazon account

Upload book to Amazon

Advertise on LDP Amazon and Facebook page

***Other services available upon request. Additional charges may apply

Lock Down Publications

P.O. Box 944

Stockbridge, GA 30281-9998

Phone # 470 303-9761

Submission Guideline

Submit the first three chapters of your completed manuscript to ldpsubmissions@gmail.com, subject line: Your book's title. The manuscript must be in a .doc file and sent as an attachment. Document should be in Times New Roman, double spaced and in size 12 font. Also, provide your synopsis and full contact information. If sending multiple submissions, they must each be in a separate email.

Have a story but no way to send it electronically? You can still submit to LDP/Ca$h Presents. Send in the first three chapters, written or typed, of your completed manuscript to:

LDP: Submissions Dept
Po Box 944
Stockbridge, Ga 30281

DO NOT send original manuscript. Must be a duplicate.

Provide your synopsis and a cover letter containing your full contact information.

Thanks for considering LDP and Ca$h Presents.

NEW RELEASES

THE STREETS NEVER LET GO 3 by ROBERT BAPTISTE

RICH $AVAGE 2 by MARTELL "TROUBLESOME" BOLDEN

A GANGSTA'S PARADISE by TRAI'QUAN

THE MURDER QUEENS 2 by MICHAEL GALLON

FOREVER GANGSTA 2 by ADRIAN DULAN

Coming Soon from Lock Down Publications/Ca$h Presents

BLOOD OF A BOSS **VI**

SHADOWS OF THE GAME II

TRAP BASTARD II

By **Askari**

LOYAL TO THE GAME **IV**

By **T.J. & Jelissa**

TRUE SAVAGE **VIII**

MIDNIGHT CARTEL IV

DOPE BOY MAGIC IV

CITY OF KINGZ III

NIGHTMARE ON SILENT AVE II

THE PLUG OF LIL MEXICO II

CLASSIC CITY II

By **Chris Green**

BLAST FOR ME **III**

A SAVAGE DOPEBOY III

CUTTHROAT MAFIA III

DUFFLE BAG CARTEL VII

HEARTLESS GOON VI

By **Ghost**

A HUSTLER'S DECEIT III

KILL ZONE II

BAE BELONGS TO ME III

TIL DEATH II

By **Aryanna**

KING OF THE TRAP III

By **T.J. Edwards**

GORILLAZ IN THE BAY V

3X KRAZY III

STRAIGHT BEAST MODE III

De'Kari

KINGPIN KILLAZ IV

STREET KINGS III

PAID IN BLOOD III

CARTEL KILLAZ IV

DOPE GODS III

Hood Rich

SINS OF A HUSTLA II

ASAD

RICH $AVAGE III

By Martell Troublesome Bolden

YAYO V

Bred In The Game 2

S. Allen

THE STREETS WILL TALK II

By Yolanda Moore

SON OF A DOPE FIEND III

HEAVEN GOT A GHETTO II

SKI MASK MONEY II

By Renta

LOYALTY AIN'T PROMISED III

By Keith Williams

I'M NOTHING WITHOUT HIS LOVE II

SINS OF A THUG II

TO THE THUG I LOVED BEFORE II

IN A HUSTLER I TRUST II

By Monet Dragun

QUIET MONEY IV

EXTENDED CLIP III

THUG LIFE IV

By **Trai'Quan**

THE STREETS MADE ME IV

By **Larry D. Wright**

IF YOU CROSS ME ONCE II

ANGEL IV

By **Anthony Fields**

THE STREETS WILL NEVER CLOSE IV

By K'ajji

HARD AND RUTHLESS III

KILLA KOUNTY III

By Khufu

MONEY GAME III

By Smoove Dolla

JACK BOYS VS DOPE BOYS II

A GANGSTA'S QUR'AN V

COKE GIRLZ II

COKE BOYS II

By Romell Tukes

MURDA WAS THE CASE II

Elijah R. Freeman

THE STREETS NEVER LET GO III

By Robert Baptiste

AN UNFORESEEN LOVE IV

By **Meesha**

KING OF THE TRENCHES III
by **GHOST & TRANAY ADAMS**

MONEY MAFIA II

By **Jibril Williams**

QUEEN OF THE ZOO III

By **Black Migo**

VICIOUS LOYALTY III

By Kingpen

A GANGSTA'S PAIN III

By J-Blunt

CONFESSIONS OF A JACKBOY III

By Nicholas Lock

GRIMEY WAYS III

By Ray Vinci

KING KILLA II

By Vincent "Vitto" Holloway

BETRAYAL OF A THUG II

By Fre$h

THE MURDER QUEENS III

By Michael Gallon

THE BIRTH OF A GANGSTER III

By Delmont Player

TREAL LOVE II

By Le'Monica Jackson

FOR THE LOVE OF BLOOD II

By Jamel Mitchell

RAN OFF ON DA PLUG II

By Paper Boi Rari

HOOD CONSIGLIERE II

By Keese

PRETTY GIRLS DO NASTY THINGS II

By Nicole Goosby

PROTÉGÉ OF A LEGEND II

By Corey Robinson

IT'S JUST ME AND YOU II

By Ah'Million
BORN IN THE GRAVE II
By Self Made Tay
FOREVER GANGSTA III
By Adrian Dulan

<u>Available Now</u>

RESTRAINING ORDER **I & II**
By **CA$H & Coffee**
LOVE KNOWS NO BOUNDARIES **I II & III**
By **Coffee**
RAISED AS A GOON I, II, III & IV
BRED BY THE SLUMS I, II, III
BLAST FOR ME I & II
ROTTEN TO THE CORE I II III
A BRONX TALE I, II, III
DUFFLE BAG CARTEL I II III IV V VI
HEARTLESS GOON I II III IV V
A SAVAGE DOPEBOY I II
DRUG LORDS I II III
CUTTHROAT MAFIA I II
KING OF THE TRENCHES
By **Ghost**
LAY IT DOWN **I & II**

LAST OF A DYING BREED I II
BLOOD STAINS OF A SHOTTA I & II III
By **Jamaica**
LOYAL TO THE GAME I II III
LIFE OF SIN I, II III
By **TJ & Jelissa**
BLOODY COMMAS I & II
SKI MASK CARTEL I II & III
KING OF NEW YORK I II,III IV V
RISE TO POWER I II III
COKE KINGS I II III IV V
BORN HEARTLESS I II III IV
KING OF THE TRAP I II
By **T.J. Edwards**
IF LOVING HIM IS WRONG…I & II
LOVE ME EVEN WHEN IT HURTS I II III
By **Jelissa**
WHEN THE STREETS CLAP BACK I & II III
THE HEART OF A SAVAGE I II III IV
MONEY MAFIA
LOYAL TO THE SOIL I II III
By **Jibril Williams**
A DISTINGUISHED THUG STOLE MY HEART I II & III
LOVE SHOULDN'T HURT I II III IV
RENEGADE BOYS I II III IV
PAID IN KARMA I II III
SAVAGE STORMS I II III
AN UNFORESEEN LOVE I II III
By **Meesha**
A GANGSTER'S CODE I &, II III

Adrian Dulan

A GANGSTER'S SYN I II III
THE SAVAGE LIFE I II III
CHAINED TO THE STREETS I II III
BLOOD ON THE MONEY I II III
A GANGSTA'S PAIN I II
By J-Blunt
PUSH IT TO THE LIMIT
By **Bre' Hayes**
BLOOD OF A BOSS **I, II, III, IV, V**
SHADOWS OF THE GAME
TRAP BASTARD
By **Askari**
THE STREETS BLEED MURDER **I, II & III**
THE HEART OF A GANGSTA I II& III
By **Jerry Jackson**
CUM FOR ME I II III IV V VI VII VIII
An **LDP Erotica Collaboration**
BRIDE OF A HUSTLA **I II & II**
THE FETTI GIRLS **I, II& III**
CORRUPTED BY A GANGSTA I, II III, IV
BLINDED BY HIS LOVE
THE PRICE YOU PAY FOR LOVE I, II ,III
DOPE GIRL MAGIC I II III
By **Destiny Skai**
WHEN A GOOD GIRL GOES BAD
By **Adrienne**
THE COST OF LOYALTY I II III
By Kweli
A GANGSTER'S REVENGE **I II III & IV**
THE BOSS MAN'S DAUGHTERS I II III IV V

212

A SAVAGE LOVE **I & II**

BAE BELONGS TO ME I II

A HUSTLER'S DECEIT I, II, III

WHAT BAD BITCHES DO I, II, III

SOUL OF A MONSTER I II III

KILL ZONE

A DOPE BOY'S QUEEN I II III

TIL DEATH

By **Aryanna**

A KINGPIN'S AMBITON

A KINGPIN'S AMBITION **II**

I MURDER FOR THE DOUGH

By **Ambitious**

TRUE SAVAGE I II III IV V VI VII

DOPE BOY MAGIC I, II, III

MIDNIGHT CARTEL I II III

CITY OF KINGZ I II

NIGHTMARE ON SILENT AVE

THE PLUG OF LIL MEXICO II

CLASSIC CITY

By **Chris Green**

A DOPEBOY'S PRAYER

By **Eddie "Wolf" Lee**

THE KING CARTEL **I, II & III**

By **Frank Gresham**

THESE NIGGAS AIN'T LOYAL **I, II & III**

By **Nikki Tee**

GANGSTA SHYT **I II &III**

By **CATO**

THE ULTIMATE BETRAYAL

Adrian Dulan

By **Phoenix**

BOSS'N UP **I , II & III**

By **Royal Nicole**

I LOVE YOU TO DEATH

By **Destiny J**

I RIDE FOR MY HITTA

I STILL RIDE FOR MY HITTA

By **Misty Holt**

LOVE & CHASIN' PAPER

By **Qay Crockett**

TO DIE IN VAIN

SINS OF A HUSTLA

By **ASAD**

BROOKLYN HUSTLAZ

By **Boogsy Morina**

BROOKLYN ON LOCK I & II

By **Sonovia**

GANGSTA CITY

By **Teddy Duke**

A DRUG KING AND HIS DIAMOND I & II III

A DOPEMAN'S RICHES

HER MAN, MINE'S TOO I, II

CASH MONEY HO'S

THE WIFEY I USED TO BE I II

PRETTY GIRLS DO NASTY THINGS

By Nicole Goosby

TRAPHOUSE KING **I II & III**

KINGPIN KILLAZ I II III

STREET KINGS I II

PAID IN BLOOD **I II**

CARTEL KILLAZ I II III

DOPE GODS I II

By **Hood Rich**

LIPSTICK KILLAH **I, II, III**

CRIME OF PASSION I II & III

FRIEND OR FOE I II III

By **Mimi**

STEADY MOBBN' **I, II, III**

THE STREETS STAINED MY SOUL I II III

By **Marcellus Allen**

WHO SHOT YA **I, II, III**

SON OF A DOPE FIEND I II

HEAVEN GOT A GHETTO

SKI MASK MONEY

Renta

GORILLAZ IN THE BAY **I II III IV**

TEARS OF A GANGSTA I II

3X KRAZY I II

STRAIGHT BEAST MODE I II

DE'KARI

TRIGGADALE I II III

MURDAROBER WAS THE CASE

Elijah R. Freeman

GOD BLESS THE TRAPPERS I, II, III

THESE SCANDALOUS STREETS I, II, III

FEAR MY GANGSTA I, II, III IV, V

THESE STREETS DON'T LOVE NOBODY I, II

BURY ME A G I, II, III, IV, V

A GANGSTA'S EMPIRE I, II, III, IV

THE DOPEMAN'S BODYGAURD I II

THE REALEST KILLAZ I II III
THE LAST OF THE OGS I II III
Tranay Adams
THE STREETS ARE CALLING
Duquie Wilson
MARRIED TO A BOSS I II III
By Destiny Skai & Chris Green
KINGZ OF THE GAME I II III IV V VI
Playa Ray
SLAUGHTER GANG I II III
RUTHLESS HEART I II III
By Willie Slaughter
FUK SHYT
By Blakk Diamond
DON'T F#CK WITH MY HEART I II
By Linnea
ADDICTED TO THE DRAMA I II III
IN THE ARM OF HIS BOSS II
By Jamila
YAYO I II III IV
A SHOOTER'S AMBITION I II
BRED IN THE GAME
By S. Allen
TRAP GOD I II III
RICH $AVAGE I II
MONEY IN THE GRAVE I II III
By Martell Troublesome Bolden
FOREVER GANGSTA I II
GLOCKS ON SATIN SHEETS I II
By Adrian Dulan

TOE TAGZ I II III IV

LEVELS TO THIS SHYT I II

IT'S JUST ME AND YOU

By Ah'Million

KINGPIN DREAMS I II III

RAN OFF ON DA PLUG

By Paper Boi Rari

CONFESSIONS OF A GANGSTA I II III IV

CONFESSIONS OF A JACKBOY I II

By Nicholas Lock

I'M NOTHING WITHOUT HIS LOVE

SINS OF A THUG

TO THE THUG I LOVED BEFORE

A GANGSTA SAVED XMAS

IN A HUSTLER I TRUST

By Monet Dragun

CAUGHT UP IN THE LIFE I II III

THE STREETS NEVER LET GO I II

By Robert Baptiste

NEW TO THE GAME I II III

MONEY, MURDER & MEMORIES I II III

By **Malik D. Rice**

LIFE OF A SAVAGE I II III

A GANGSTA'S QUR'AN I II III IV

MURDA SEASON I II III

GANGLAND CARTEL I II III

CHI'RAQ GANGSTAS I II III

KILLERS ON ELM STREET I II III

JACK BOYZ N DA BRONX I II III

A DOPEBOY'S DREAM I II III

Adrian Dulan

JACK BOYS VS DOPE BOYS
COKE GIRLZ
COKE BOYS
By Romell Tukes
LOYALTY AIN'T PROMISED I II
By Keith Williams
QUIET MONEY I II III
THUG LIFE I II III
EXTENDED CLIP I II
A GANGSTA'S PARADISE
By **Trai'Quan**
THE STREETS MADE ME I II III
By **Larry D. Wright**
THE ULTIMATE SACRIFICE I, II, III, IV, V, VI
KHADIFI
IF YOU CROSS ME ONCE
ANGEL I II III
IN THE BLINK OF AN EYE
By **Anthony Fields**
THE LIFE OF A HOOD STAR
By Ca$h & Rashia Wilson
THE STREETS WILL NEVER CLOSE I II III
By K'ajji
CREAM I II III
THE STREETS WILL TALK
By Yolanda Moore
NIGHTMARES OF A HUSTLA I II III
By King Dream
CONCRETE KILLA I II III
VICIOUS LOYALTY I II

By Kingpen

HARD AND RUTHLESS I II

MOB TOWN 251

THE BILLIONAIRE BENTLEYS I II III

By Von Diesel

GHOST MOB

Stilloan Robinson

MOB TIES I II III IV V VI

SOUL OF A HUSTLER, HEART OF A KILLER

By SayNoMore

BODYMORE MURDERLAND I II III

THE BIRTH OF A GANGSTER I II

By Delmont Player

FOR THE LOVE OF A BOSS

By C. D. Blue

MOBBED UP I II III IV

THE BRICK MAN I II III IV

THE COCAINE PRINCESS I II III IV V

By King Rio

KILLA KOUNTY I II III

By Khufu

MONEY GAME I II

By Smoove Dolla

A GANGSTA'S KARMA I II

By FLAME

KING OF THE TRENCHES I II

by **GHOST & TRANAY ADAMS**

QUEEN OF THE ZOO I II

By **Black Migo**

GRIMEY WAYS I II

By Ray Vinci

XMAS WITH AN ATL SHOOTER

By Ca$h & Destiny Skai

KING KILLA

By Vincent "Vitto" Holloway

BETRAYAL OF A THUG

By Fre$h

THE MURDER QUEENS I II

By Michael Gallon

TREAL LOVE

By Le'Monica Jackson

FOR THE LOVE OF BLOOD

By Jamel Mitchell

HOOD CONSIGLIERE

By Keese

PROTÉGÉ OF A LEGEND

By Corey Robinson

BORN IN THE GRAVE

By Self Made Tay

MOAN IN MY MOUTH

By XTASY

BOOKS BY LDP'S CEO, CA$H

TRUST IN NO MAN

TRUST IN NO MAN 2

TRUST IN NO MAN 3

BONDED BY BLOOD

SHORTY GOT A THUG

THUGS CRY

THUGS CRY 2

THUGS CRY 3

TRUST NO BITCH

TRUST NO BITCH 2

TRUST NO BITCH 3

TIL MY CASKET DROPS

RESTRAINING ORDER

RESTRAINING ORDER 2

IN LOVE WITH A CONVICT

LIFE OF A HOOD STAR

XMAS WITH AN ATL SHOOTER

Adrian Dulan

www.ingramcontent.com/pod-product-compliance
Lightning Source LLC
Chambersburg PA
CBHW070454260626
47161CB00004B/1302